Dear Reader,

As I write my books, my hero and heroine become very real to me. I laugh with them, I cry with them... and I try to give them everything they need to ensure their story will have a happy-ever-after ending. But when my hero in this book, Zack Alexander, told me he wanted me to buy him a star, I was afraid he'd set me an impossible task!

Then fate led me to the Vancouver Pacific Space Center, where I found I could indeed "buy" a star through their fund-raising program. I held my breath till I learned that my special star for Zack was still available. Then I "bought" and registered it, and the official Star Deed now hangs in a place of honor in my office.

When you read Zack and Lauren's story, you'll find out why Zack wanted this very special star, and I hope it will bring a warm glow to your heart, just as it did to mine!

Best wishes,

Grace Green

Grace Green was born in Scotland and is a former teacher. In 1967 she and her marine engineer husband, John, immigrated to Canada where they raised their four children. Grace is now happily settled in West Vancouver in a house overlooking the ocean. She enjoys walking the seawall, gardening, getting together with other writers... and watching her characters come to life, because she knows that once they do, they will take over and write her stories for her.

Books by Grace Green

HARLEQUIN ROMANCE®
3526—THE WEDDING PROMISE
3542—BRANNIGAN'S BABY

Don't miss any of our special offers. Write to us at the following address for information on our newest releases.

Harlequin Reader Service
U.S.: 3010 Walden Ave., P.O. Box 1325, Buffalo, NY 14269
Canadian: P.O. Box 609, Fort Erie, Ont. L2A 5X3

New Year...
New Family
Grace Green

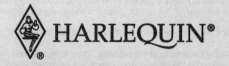

TORONTO • NEW YORK • LONDON
AMSTERDAM • PARIS • SYDNEY • HAMBURG
STOCKHOLM • ATHENS • TOKYO • MILAN • MADRID
PRAGUE • WARSAW • BUDAPEST • AUCKLAND

In loving memory of Sarah Margaret Reid

ISBN 0-373-03586-1

NEW YEAR...NEW FAMILY

First North American Publication 2000.

Copyright © 1998 by Grace Green.

Visit us at www.romance.net

Printed in U.S.A.

CHAPTER ONE

"HEY, man, *great* party!"

Zack Alexander faked a smile as he glanced at the bleary-eyed guest weaving by with a glass of Scotch and a giggling redhead. "Thanks, buddy. Glad you're having fun."

Everybody seemed to be enjoying his pre-Christmas shindig, he mused—everybody except the host himself. *He* was bored out of his skull and wished they'd all go home.

Especially the voluptuous brunette who had, ten minutes ago, attached herself to him with the relentless dedication of a sex-starved octopus. He made another determined effort to disentangle himself from—what the devil was her name again? Melissa? Clarissa? Alyssia?

"Honey." He grasped her wrists firmly and eased her fingers from his hair. "You'll have to excuse me. I do believe I hear the phone ringing next door in my study."

She slid her arms under his silk-lined Armani jacket. Dipped her fingertips boldly beneath the waistband of his trousers. Tugged up his shirttail.

Desperately, he worked himself free of her tentacles.

"Excuse me, Melissa—" he shoved his shirt in and avoiding her reaching hands, stepped away from her "—I must get the phone. It could be a business call, my manager."

"It's Alyssia!" she called after him sulkily.

He rolled his eyes as he reached his study. Whatever!

Shutting the door behind him, he heaved out a thankful sigh and, shaking his head, wandered to his desk.

He'd lied, of course. He hadn't heard the phone. Besides, Jerry Macinaw, general manager of Alexander Electronics, never phoned the boss at home. He paged him.

But somebody had called since he was in here earlier in the day, and had left a message. The red light on the answering machine was blinking furiously.

Frowning, he hit the black button.

"Mr Alexander." The voice was female and brisk. "My name is Donna. It's five-thirty, Thursday, December seventeenth. I'm calling for Tyler Braddock of Braddock, Braddock and Black, barristers and solicitors. Mr. Braddock would like to meet with you in his office tomorrow morning at eleven on a matter of some urgency. Could you please call and leave a message with our answering service to confirm if this time will be convenient? Thank you."

Tyler Braddock?

Zack scowled. He'd never heard of the man.

Hitching his lean hip on the edge of his desk, he swept back a swathe of jet-black hair with his right hand while with his left he picked up the phone.

Nothing smelled sweeter than success!

Lauren Alexander's blue eyes glowed with satisfaction as she walked into her luxury condo's marble-floored foyer.

An hour ago she'd been offered a plum promotion. Her employer, Jack Perrini of the Perrini Life Insurance Agency, had given her a couple of weeks off to mull the offer over—as if she needed a couple of weeks! But he'd insisted.

"You haven't taken a break in almost three years," he'd said. And added confidently, "When you come back in the new year, you'll be ready to make the move to Toronto and take over as general manager of our Ontario branch."

She hadn't been sure till the last minute that she'd get the job. Angela Marwick had been a close contender. But though Angie's sales record was as good as Lauren's, Angie was a single mother with a child in kindergarten, and Jack had more than hinted that Lauren's status—unattached with no dependents—had been the deciding factor in his decision.

She shrugged off her black coat, draped it over an armchair in the sitting room and went straight to the kitchen. She opened the fridge and whisked out the mini-bottle of Brut she'd bought on spec for just this occasion.

"To success!" she declared a moment later as the bubbly foamed into one of her crystal fluted glasses.

To success! Her triumphant toast echoed at her from the pristine white-painted walls.

It had a hollow sound.

Brusquely she dismissed the unsettling thought.

Taking quick sips from her glass, she wandered around her condo, deliberately savoring the peace and quiet, admiring the starkly sophisticated decor, enjoying the panoramic view of Vancouver from the wide bay window.

It wasn't till she was on her way to the kitchen that she noticed the winking red light on the answering machine on the hall table.

She paused, hit the white button.

"Ms. Alexander." The voice was female and brisk. "My name is Donna. It's five thirty-five, Thursday, December seventeenth. I'm calling for Tyler Braddock of Braddock, Braddock and Black, barristers and solicitors. Mr. Braddock would like to meet with you in his office tomorrow morning at eleven on a matter of some urgency. Could you please call and leave a message with our answering service to confirm if this time will be convenient? Thank you."

Tyler Braddock. Lauren frowned. She'd never heard of the man.

Sinking gracefully onto the chair beside the phone table, she ran a smoothing hand over her upswept blond hair while with the other she picked up the phone.

At five to eleven on Friday, December eighteenth, Zack Alexander swung his scarlet Porsche into the last vacant spot in Braddock, Braddock and Black's above-ground parking lot in downtown Vancouver. To his left was a white Mercedes that had glided into place ten seconds ahead of him.

As he switched off the ignition, the driver of the Mercedes emerged and stepped smartly toward the front door of the pink granite high-rise building.

Through his side window he caught a peekaboo glimpse of severely styled ash-blond hair. The haughty swing of a calf-length black coat. The flash of pale stockings.

He uncoiled himself from the Porsche and walked at a more leisurely pace toward the high-rise, enjoying the crisp cold of the day and the breeze that whipped his cheeks.

Inside the building, the foyer was deserted. He crossed

to the bank of elevators and pressed the up button. Glancing idly along the corridor, he saw the blond stranger disappearing into the ladies' room.

Probably checking to see that not a hair was out of place, he reflected. He could tell by the arrogant way she walked that she was as uptight as they came. If there was one thing he detested it was a ramrod rigid woman!

He had to wait a good three minutes before an elevator deigned to descend, and it was with a feeling of impatience that he entered it and pressed the button for the nineteenth floor.

The doors were closing when he heard the click-click-click of high heels approaching fast. A voice called, ''Hold it!'' He obeyed, and in a blur of motion the blonde slipped past him with a breathless 'Thanks.'''

He released the door and it glided into place. ''Floor?'' he asked without looking around. His hand hovered at the panel of buttons.

'Nineteen.''

He dropped his arm. So, she was going to the same floor as he was. Was she a lawyer? Did she perhaps work for Braddock, Braddock and Black?

Her perfume lingered in his space. The scent was sophisticated and expensive. Bold and confident. Entirely suitable, he decided, for a successful career woman.

He suddenly felt a compelling urge to turn and look at her face. He resisted. She wasn't his type, he could tell that from her perfume. Too cold, too...distant. His taste ran to something more romantic, passionate.

Shoving his hands into the slash pockets of his leather jacket, he leaned a shoulder against the side wall and kept his gaze fixed on the ascending numbers above the door.

Five, six, seven, eight...

*   *   *

Lauren stared aghast at the back of her husband's head.

Estranged husband, she corrected herself numbly, as she sagged against the wall. More than three years since she'd walked away from their marriage. More than three years since she'd set eyes on him. What perverse quirk of fate had brought him here at this exact moment?

He hadn't realized who she was. Yet. But he would stand aside to let her exit the elevator ahead of him. Was it possible she could get by without being recognized?

She tried to drag her gaze from him, but dammit, it stubbornly feasted on every well-remembered inch, from the silky black hair to the broad shoulders to the long, powerful legs to the size-eleven feet. The black leather jacket was new, the blue jeans were old, the Nikes were scuffed. The total package was every woman's fantasy.

He was whistling through his teeth, a habit she'd teased him about often in days gone by. Memories tore at her heart. Ruthlessly she fought them off.

The elevator jolted to a halt. The door glided open.

Legs threatening to buckle, she stepped around him, keeping her face averted. She'd never worn her hair in this sophisticated style when they'd been together. Nor had she ever dressed so formally. With a bit of luck she'd—

"Lauren?"

Escape. But this was *not*, obviously, going to be her lucky day, and she just as obviously was *not* going to escape.

The elevator door closed behind them as they stood facing each other in the plushly carpeted corridor.

"Zack. This is a...surprise."

And some. She hoped her dismay didn't show. He looked older than his thirty years. Those deep grooves etched on either side of his mouth shocked her almost as much as the bleak emptiness in his gray eyes, an emptiness that was swiftly veiled as he ran an assessing gaze over her.

"I wouldn't have known you," he said softly, "if I'd passed you on the street. You look different, Lauren."

"Time has that effect on people." She flicked the narrow cuff of her coat sleeve and glanced at the white face of her gold and silver watch. "Now if you'll excuse me—"

"Have you time for a coffee when—"

"I'm sorry." Brusquely she dropped her cuff. "I really have to rush—I have an appointment at eleven."

She turned and strode along the narrow corridor, praying she was going in the right direction. Anxiously, she scanned the names on the doors, and with a trembling relief saw Braddock, Braddock and Black painted on the dimpled glass of the door ahead, to her right.

Because of the plush carpeting, her heels had made no sound as she hurried toward the door, but because of the plush carpeting, she'd been unable to hear Zack and didn't know he was right behind her till she reached out for the brass knob and he got there first.

"Allow me!" With a flourish, he opened the door and stood aside to let her pass.

"Thank you," she said stiffly. But when he followed her into the empty waiting room, she swiveled and frowned at him.

"About that coffee," he said, "how about meeting after your appointment—"

"I'd appreciate," she said, "if you'd stop following me."

She whirled from him and strode to the receptionist's desk. "Lauren Alexander," she announced in a clear voice. "I have an eleven o'clock appointment with Tyler Braddock."

"Please have a seat. I'll let Mr. Braddock know you're here."

Lauren turned, and her heartbeats jarred when she saw Zack hadn't gone. Ignoring him, she stalked to a couch at the far end of the waiting room...and felt her nervousness escalate when he strolled across and took a seat right beside her. She smelled the familiar musky smell of his hair mingled with the spicy fragrance of his cologne.

Her senses swooned. She wanted to fall into his arms.

"Zack—" deliberately she peeled off one leather glove, "we have nothing to say to each other. Please go. Unless you want me to make a scene."

"The Lauren I knew didn't make scenes."

"The Lauren you knew no longer exists." She peeled off the other glove, tucked both into her black purse. "Three years is a long time. People do change." She leveled a cool gaze at him.

He blinked first.

"Yeah." His tone was flat. "I guess they do. Forget about the coffee...it was a bad idea."

She waited for him to rise and leave. Instead, he sank back, crossed one leg over the other and stared with an appearance of concentrated interest at an oil painting of the totem poles in Stanley Park. Before she could protest his continued presence, a door opened to the right of the reception desk and a man appeared. He was tall and bald and bespectacled and dressed in a navy pin-striped suit.

''Ah, Mr. and Mrs. Alexander.'' He waved them forward. ''Come right in.''

Lauren did a mental double take. He wanted to see Zack, too? What on earth was going on? Was Zack behind this summons to the lawyer's office?

But for what purpose?

Divorce.

The answer slammed into her mind so savagely she almost winced. *Of course.* How could she have been so dumb! Zack must want his freedom, and he'd arranged this meeting for the purpose of setting proceedings in motion.

She felt sick as the lawyer took her coat and Zack's jacket and hung them on a coatrack just inside his office door. Zack must have met someone else, must have fallen in love...

And planned to remarry.

She'd known—in a secret corner of her heart she'd always known—that one day this moment would come.

But she wasn't ready for it.

She would never be ready for it.

The office had a fabulous view of Coal Harbour and the North Shore mountains. On any other occasion, Zack might have made an appreciative comment. Right now he was far too busy wondering why Lauren's face had become chalk white when the lawyer had greeted them.

And as she took one of the seats angled in front of the wide teak desk, he found himself wondering if she knew something he didn't.

Well, he'd find out soon enough. Through narrowed

eyes, he watched the lawyer lower his angular body into the teak swivel chair on the other side of the desk.

The man set his elbows on the arms of his chair, steepled his fingers under his chin.

"You must both be wondering," he said, "why I had my secretary call and ask you to come here. Let me explain. Something rather...odd...has happened. I've been contacted by a Los Angeles law firm regarding—" He twitched his glasses onto the bridge of his nose. "You were, I believe, close friends of the late Mac and Lisa Smith?"

The *late* Mac and Lisa Smith?

Shocked, Zack said, "Mac and Lisa are..."

"You didn't know? Oh, dear, I am sorry." The lawyer tut-tutted. "Six months ago, Mr. and Mrs. Smith perished when fire swept through their suburban home."

Zack swiveled in his chair and stared at Lauren. "Did you know?" His voice sounded rough.

She shook her head. He saw her swallow as if something had lodged in her throat. But not a tear glistened in her eyes, not a quiver made her lips tremble. Attagirl, he thought bitterly. Don't for God's sake let anything make a crack in that wall of ice that's frozen around your heart.

He'd believed he'd gotten over the anger, but as it exploded afresh in a blinding, crimson flame, he realized it had been simmering just under the surface all this while, ready to flare up anew at the slightest provocation.

Fire and ice.

His fire. Her ice.

He wanted to see just one tiny fissure mar that cool, smooth facade.

He wanted to smash his fist on the desk in front of him.

He wanted to weep.

He lunged to his feet and crossed to the window, stood with his back to them both.

He stared out, not seeing what was ahead, seeing only the past.

Mac and Lisa, once their closest friends, married the same summer as he and Lauren.

Arabella, Mac and Lisa's daughter, born the same month and in the same hospital as—

Shuddering, he closed his eyes against the threatening tears. Get a grip, Alexander! For God's sake, get a grip.

He exhaled, counted to ten. To twenty. And turned.

"Their little girl." He avoided looking at Lauren. "Was she..."

"Ah, Arabella." The lawyer lifted a hand, gestured toward Zack's chair. Feeling as if the floor was tilting under him, Zack sat down. Not once did he look at Lauren.

"That is why I called this meeting," Tyler Braddock said. "I'm happy to tell you Arabella is alive and well. She was staying at a friend's place the night of the fire—"

"Thank God!" Zack said with heart-felt vehemence.

"And since her parents' death, the little eight-year-old has been in the care of her only living relative, her great-aunt Dolly."

"Dolly Smith?" Zack shook his head in disbelief.

"You know her?" the lawyer asked.

"And some! If ever a woman was misnamed it was that one. Dolly Smith is a desiccated old bitch who's—"

"Mr. Braddock," Lauren cut in, "this news of Mac

and Lisa's deaths is extremely distressing and I am, of course, relieved to hear that their child is safe. What I don't understand is why you've asked me to come here this morning. I haven't been in contact with the Smiths for years.''

''I'm just coming to that, Mrs. Alexander. It was the will, you see, or rather, the lack thereof.'' The lawyer twitched his glasses again. ''The fire totally destroyed the Smiths' property, and with it, all their records. The executor advertised widely and for months, but it is only recently that any will was located. In Vancouver, actually, in a safety deposit box at one of the downtown banks.''

''They lived here at one time,'' Zack explained. ''But have you called us in just to tell us that the Smiths have bequeathed us some small memento?'' Surely a note in the mail would have done the job, he reflected with impatience.

''A small memento?'' A flicker of amusement crossed the lawyer's face. ''Yes, you could say that. A small memento. Oh, yes, that's rich.'' He chuckled as if at some private joke.

Lauren glanced pointedly at her watch. ''Mr. Braddock—''

''Forgive me, my dear, for wanting to savor the moment of drama. I have here a copy of that will—'' he scooped a file from the desk in front of him ''—and I shall now read out to you the pertinent paragraph. Tada, tada, tada—ah, here we are. 'And we, Mac and Lisa Smith, do hereby declare that in the event that we should both die without leaving one or other as survivor, guardianship of our beloved daughter, Arabella, should fall to our dearest friends Zack and Lauren Alexander.'''

For a moment, Zack couldn't take it in. When he did, he felt as dizzy as if he'd been rocketed around on a jet-propelled carousel. Then the dizzy feeling faded, and as it did, emotions scrambled around in his heart, each seeking the dominant position.

He'd lost touch with Mac and Lisa, but he'd never stopped caring about them. And he would grieve over their loss. But he'd coped with grief before. He could cope again. Now he must think of Arabella.

In a corner of his heart, a corner he'd thought dead, he felt the faint stirring of hope.

He turned to Lauren, a tentative smile in his eyes. A smile that died when he saw her frozen expression.

Ignoring him, she pushed herself to her feet.

"Mr. Braddock." She clutched her bag with white-knuckled hands. "That will was written eight years ago, at a time when Zack and I were married—"

"We're still married, Lauren," Zack interjected softly.

"In name only! You and I have been separated for more than three years! In fact I thought—when Mr Braddock called us into his office just now—that the reason for this meeting was you were going to set divorce proceedings in motion." She swung her attention to the lawyer. "At any rate, there's no room in my life for a child. If Zack decides to bring up Arabella, he'll have to do it alone."

Zack lurched to his feet as she made for the door. But as she grabbed her coat and opened the door, he restrained himself from trying to detain her.

She'd said there was no room in her life for a child. She might as well have said there was no room in her life for love, because that was what she really meant.

Why, in God's name, had he allowed himself to hope, even for one fleeting moment, that he would ever see the faintest thawing of that frozen heart?

The door slammed behind her.

Tyler Braddock cleared his throat. "Er, Mr. Alexander?"

Zack turned with an apologetic gesture and faced the lawyer. "Mr. Braddock, you have to understand—"

"Oh, I do, I do," the man hastened to say. "It would be...difficult, to say the least, for you and your estranged wife to become joint guardians. And I gather, from Mrs. Alexander's attitude, that she doesn't like children."

"That's where you're quite wrong," Zack said, feeling as if he were drowning in sorrow. "She loves children."

"Then why..."

"We had a child. A little girl. She died when she was four, and my wife has never gotten over it."

CHAPTER TWO

LAUREN stumbled into the main floor ladies' room and staggered to the nearest sink. She fumbled for the cold tap, turned it on fully and scooped up handful after handful of icy water, splashing it into her face till she gasped.

And all the time, her stomach muscles heaved, dry, convulsive retchings. Dear God, it was too much, first seeing Zack, then the devastating news about Mac and Lisa.

And the final blow, the blow that had made her want to cry out with the pain of it. Arabella. Mac and Lisa had never changed their will. The will they'd made eight years ago. The will that had designated Zack and her as joint guardians for their little girl.

Oh, the unbearable cruelty of fate.

But crueler than that had been the expression of hope she'd seen in Zack's eyes when he'd turned to her. She'd always been able to read him like an open book. What she'd seen there, at that moment, had sent a chill down her spine. He saw Arabella as some kind of a miracle that had come into their lives and would bring them together.

It wasn't going to happen.

She would never allow Mac and Lisa's daughter into her life, because that would mean taking her into her heart. And she would never allow herself to love a child again because that would make her vulnerable to the

19

kind of pain she'd suffered when Becky died. She wasn't about to take that risk.

Craven?

Yes, she was craven.

It was her weakness and it was her shame.

And it was the only way she knew to survive.

She reached with trembling hands for a paper towel, and with her gaze fixed on her ashen face, patted her cheeks dry. Her lipstick was blurred. Roughly she rubbed her mouth with the paper towel, then extricated her cosmetic bag, and a comb, from her purse.

It took her several minutes to fix her face and tidy her hair. Then, satisfied that her exterior, at least, showed no signs of her breakdown, she left the ladies' room.

Zack would still be with the lawyer, she reassured herself as she hurried along the corridor. There would be many things to discuss, arrangements to be made, forms to fill in and sign.

But when she went into the parking lot, there he was, leaning against her Mercedes.

At the sight of him, a shock wave of attraction slammed into her. She steeled herself to resist it as he pushed himself from the vehicle and came toward her.

"How did you know that was my car?" she asked.

"I saw you arrive. Look, there's a Starbucks just around the corner. We have to talk."

"We have nothing to—"

He placed his hand firmly against the small of her back and walked her toward the street. She sensed that in the mood he was in, if she tried to take off he'd sweep her up in his arms and carry her. Discretion, in this case, was obviously the better part of valor.

Though the coffee shop was crowded, Zack found two

empty stools at the counter. He ordered cappuccinos but didn't initiate conversation till the counter clerk had slid their coffees in front of them and moved away.

Then he hooked an ankle around the low bar of his stool, and as she sipped from her mug, he looked at her steadily.

"Lauren." His tone was low, non-confrontational. "You can't keep running like this."

"Who says I'm running?" Over the rim of her mug, she stared at him challengingly.

"I do." A wispy lace of hot milk froth hovered on her upper lip. What would she do, he wondered, if he leaned over and kissed it away? Slap him, probably. "You're running from responsibility. We agreed, you and I, to be named as Arabella's guardians in Mac and Lisa's will. It was a reciprocal thing, they did the same for us."

"Mac and Lisa knew we'd separated. It was their responsibility to change their will."

"Sure it was. But they obviously let it slide. People do. Have you updated your will?" he asked bluntly.

"No, but that's different."

"How different?" he persisted.

She stared into her mug. "Don't do this, Zack."

"How is it different?" He repeated his question in a quiet voice.

Features set tightly, she continued to stare into her mug.

"Because our child is dead?"

Her gaze flew to his, and for a split second he thought he saw a glimmer of tears.

Then she put down her mug, scooped up her bag, swung off her stool. And before he could blink, she'd rushed away through the crowds at the entrance, and before he'd taken two steps after her she'd disappeared.

Damn!

Excusing himself right and left, he worked his way to the door and raced to the street. Just in time to see her running to the car park.

He caught up with her when she was just a few meters from the Mercedes. He grabbed her arm, made her turn to face him.

"I'm not finished," he said.

"Please let me go!" Her cheeks were flushed, a few strands of her hair had come loose, and her eyes were as panicky as those of a deer trapped by roaring flames.

"You should have waited," he said grimly, "to hear the rest of what Tyler Braddock had to say."

"I'm not interested in—"

"Dolly Smith sent Arabella to boarding school just three weeks after the fire. Three weeks after she'd lost her parents, for God's sake! When she needed love and affection and security more than anything in the world! Lauren, your father shunted you off to boarding school after your mother died—"

"It's history, Zack."

"Yeah, history. But it's been repeated here, and we, you and I together, can put a stop to it. That poor kid must be going through hell. Not only has she lost her parents, she's been uprooted from her school, her friends, and dumped in a situation where—"

She wrenched her arm free and glared at him. "It's not my responsibility, Zack!"

He took a step back and looked at her. Her eyes were sparking, no longer panicky, and her chin had a defiant thrust. She was barely recognizable as the woman who had once loved with such tender passion.

The woman who had borne and cherished their child.

He held up his hands in surrender. "You're absolutely right." He sighed. "Arabella isn't your responsibility."

Did her features relax? Just a little? Yeah, he was letting her off the hook, he thought bitterly. She could go back to her ordered little life with a clear conscience.

"Mac and Lisa should have updated their wills. That they didn't was surely an oversight." He slid his hands into his jacket pockets. "But Mac was my best buddy from the time we were in kindergarten, and I'm not about to let him down. I've arranged with Tyler Braddock to have Arabella fly up here for the holidays. She'll be arriving tomorrow afternoon. We'll spend the next couple of weeks together. A probation period, as it were. And if she likes it here, if she wants to stay with me, I'll apply for permanent custody."

Lauren's eyelids flickered, but she gave no other sign that his announcement had affected her.

"Won't that put a crimp in your social life?" There was just the faintest hint of sarcasm in her tone. "All those wild parties you throw—they've become a regular feature in the *Sun*'s society column."

"My life has been empty since you left." He saw her neck muscles tighten. God, he had to admire her self-control. "Arabella's life, I imagine, is pretty empty, too. Perhaps we can help each other find some joy again."

Tension shimmered between them like quivering silken threads.

Then, taking him completely by surprise, she reached up and gently touched his cheek. "You're a good man,

Zack," she whispered. "I wish you nothing but the best."

He covered her hand with one of his. "Lauren." His voice was husky. "Won't you please—"

She pulled away from him, and a moment later she was in her car. The door clicked shut. He saw her lock it.

Without looking at him again, she backed out of the parking spot and drove the Mercedes smoothly away.

Out of the parking lot. Out of his life.

Again.

Leaving him standing alone, shoulders slumped, eyes blurred. And even more lonely and filled with despair than he'd been on the day she'd walked out of their marriage.

That night, Lauren had trouble sleeping.

When she eventually drifted off, after tossing and turning for hours, it was close to dawn. And her sleep was disturbed by nightmares.

Nightmares dominated at first by the mean face and embittered words of Dolly Smith. Words flung at a weeping Arabella, who ran and ran and kept on running....

Then the nightmare changed. It was no longer Arabella who was running, but Lauren, as a seven-year-old child, lost in the maze of corridors at St. Elizabeth's School for Girls, lost and terrified and looking desperately for a mother who was nowhere to be found.

With a violent jerk, she woke and lurched to a sitting position. Her silk nightie was soaked, her body limp. She shivered, threw back her covers and got up.

She crossed to the window, flicked back the pale curtains and stared out at the morning. The city streets were already abustle. The eastern sky was streaked with pink, and to the west the waters of English Bay were a muted charcoal gray. It was going to be a lovely day.

And this afternoon Zack would go to the airport to pick up Arabella.

Zack.

If her heart wasn't already broken, it would have broken yesterday when she'd touched his cheek, looked into his eyes and seen the anguish there.

Just when she was beginning to look to the future, just when her career was beginning to take off, he had come back into her life, his presence threatening to destroy her hard-won and still shaky equilibrium.

Thank heaven she'd be leaving for Toronto in the new year.

Running! his voice mocked her. *Running, running, running!*

Slicing a hand angrily, dismissively through the air, she closed her mind to the jarring accusation.

She wasn't running.

She was moving on.

There was a difference.

''For pity's sake, Mrs. Potter, don't desert me in my hour of need! How can I bring a child—'' Zack flung out his right arm in a desperate gesture that swept the entire sitting room ''—into this?''

His once-a-week housekeeper's outraged gaze skimmed the chaos. Dirty glasses. Teeming ashtrays. Plates caked with dried food. Carpet littered with party detritus including wrappers labeled Fine Time Takeout

Pizzas and smeared with gobs of what could be either catsup or blood.

She exploded. "Mr. Alexander, I told you last week I'd quit if you didn't stop these wild parties! For the same money you give me I can spend my Saturdays cleaning a sweet little bungalow in Kitsilano where the nastiest thing I might find under the cushions would be a chocolate wrapper!"

Groveling. That was what was called for here. Zack placed his right hand over his heart and adopted his most ingratiating smile. "No more parties, Mrs. P. I swear. And a raise. Plus a stupendous Christmas bonus."

"Mr. Alexander." She unwrapped the floral apron tied around her ample girth. "You need help."

"Up until a second ago, I thought I had it!"

"I'm not talking about your house." Fastidiously, she folded the apron. "I'm talking about your soul." She fixed him with a gaze so fierce it would have stared down an eagle. "What you're looking for you're not going to find at your wild parties, and that's for sure!"

He spread his hands in a beseeching gesture. "Mrs. P., I don't even *enjoy* these parties!"

"Then why do you have them?" She sliced her glance toward an area on the wall above the fireplace, pursed her lips, shook her head.

He followed her gaze and saw what he hadn't noticed before, a Rorschach stain that looked to him like a man hanging from a gallows. How it had gotten there, he hadn't a clue, but it appeared as if someone had thrown a Hawaiian pizza slice at his Izzard oil painting and had—thank heavens—missed.

Why have them? Mrs. Potter's question echoed in his head. *To fill up the space in my heart,* he could have told her. And he didn't need help—at least, not the kind to which she was referring. He would work things out in his own way, as he'd been doing for the past four years.

It's not happening! an inner voice mocked him.

It will! he answered defiantly.

Mrs. Potter slung her bulky bag over her shoulder. "Goodbye, Mr. Alexander."

She turned and made for the door.

On her way out she stopped automatically to straighten one of the cushions on the chesterfield. He heard a hiss as she scooped something up.

Oh, hell! He grimaced as he saw it was a flimsy black bra. How it had gotten there, he had no idea.

She turned and looked at him. And then dropped the bra onto the carpet as if it had burned her fingers.

He stood there, cursing under his breath, till the back door slammed shut behind her.

Then he blew out a sigh and glanced at his watch. If he got a move on, he could possibly have the sitting room shipshape before he left for the airport.

With his hands on his hips, he scanned the area bleakly, his gaze catching on the pizza stain above the fireplace. That, he decided, was the place to start.

He got himself a bucket of hot soapy water and a sponge. He dragged a bentwood chair from the kitchen and hauled it to the left side of the fireplace under the stain.

He set the bucket on the cream marble hearth. He dipped the yellow sponge into the water and wrung it out.

He stood on the chair. He hitched his right knee on the marble mantelpiece, and balancing with the tip of his left shoe on the chair, stretched as far as he could with the sponge. The stain was within reach. But just. Another couple of inches, and he'd have had to go to the garden shed and fetch a damned ladder!

Grunting, he started scrubbing.

Lauren was in the kitchen after a late lunch, rinsing a sprig of purple grapes under the tap, when the phone rang.

She put down the grapes, dried her fingertips on a forest green and ecru embroidered Christmas hand towel, crossed to the wall phone and picked up the receiver.

"Hello?"

"Thank heavens you're at home!"

"Zack." She leaned weakly against the wall. "You're wasting your time. I'm not interested in—"

"Lauren, I need your help."

"No." She could hear a hubbub of noise in the background. Was he calling from the airport? Had he somehow missed Arabella? Despite herself, she felt a stab of concern. "Where are you calling from?"

No answer for a beat. And then, tersely, "Emergency."

She straightened. "Hospital?"

"Vancouver General."

Her fingers clawed the receiver. "Zack, what's wrong?"

"Broken ankle, nothing too serious, but dammit, I'm stuck here till they get around to setting it, and Lord only knows when that'll be! There's been a major pileup on the Squamish highway, and this place is a madhouse. Lauren, Arabella's plane is due in just over an hour."

She imagined him raking a hand through his black hair

the way he always did when he was distraught. "There's no way I'm going to make it. I know what I'm asking, but..."

She stared out the kitchen window. A brown-speckled sea gull swooped by, crying out with an angry sound. Her throat felt dry. She found it difficult to speak. "Surely there's someone else you can ask..."

"They won't hand an unaccompanied minor over to just anybody, for Pete's sake!"

"Can't you call the airport, tell them what's happened?"

"They're not about to take the word of somebody over the phone! Look, as designated guardians, both our names are on the release form that'll be traveling with her. One of us has to be there to pick her up. Otherwise..."

She could almost see his helpless shrug.

Her thoughts swirled, desperately swirled. "I don't really have a choice now, do I." The words came out tonelessly. A statement. Not a question.

"Oh, God, thank you, sweetheart."

Goose bumps rose on her arms. Sweetheart. Nobody else had ever called her that. She wanted to cry.

She cleared her throat and answered him in her most businesslike tone.

"Zack, I'll go to the airport and meet Arabella. And I'll take her to my place. Call me when you get home and I'll deliver her to you. After that you're on your own."

"You make it sound as if you're delivering a box of groceries."

"Just give me the details—flight number, time of arrival."

She could hardly hear his voice over the racket in the background, someone screaming, someone cursing at high pitch.

"Got that?" he asked.

"Yes. I'll see you later then. And Zack..."

"Yeah?"

"I know how you hate hospitals. Hang tough!"

Replacing the receiver, she realized her hand had become slick with perspiration. And the kitchen, all of a sudden, seemed stiflingly hot. She murmured a sound of frustration. If she hadn't spent so much time that morning at the travel agent's, planning her Toronto trip, she'd have already left for her walk and would have escaped Zack's call.

Her lips twisted in a derisive smile as she opened the patio door and stepped onto the small balcony. She shivered as the cool wind cut through her sweater, but she welcomed its bracing blast.

She lifted her head and sniffed. The weather was changing. She could smell snow in the air. The sky was smudged with dirty-looking gray clouds. And ten stories below, the very last scurries of autumn leaves danced in gusts across the sidewalks.

The wrought-iron railing was rough under her fingers as she curled her hands around it.

Arabella.

Somewhere at Lindenlea—probably still in the TV armoire in the den unless Zack had moved it—was a video containing several shots of the child. But she didn't need any video to remind herself of what Mac and Lisa's daughter looked like in order to recognize her at the airport.

Arabella would still be tall and skinny. Her curly hair

would still be the same carroty red, her wide-spaced eyes the same apple green. And she would still be the image of her mother, as she always had been, even to the funny pointed ears and the freckles on her tip-tilted nose.

Becky, on the other hand, had taken after her father. She'd been the image of Zack.

Lauren shivered again. She unwrapped her fingers from the railing, hugged her arms around herself and stood a while longer. Finally, after a glance at her watch, she went inside.

She'd have to leave soon for the airport.

Zack gritted his teeth as the doctor manipulated his ankle. The last place he wanted to be right now was flat on his back on this gurney, wearing nothing but a skimpy buttercup yellow wraparound dress!

And with another man running warm hands up and down his hairy leg.

"What happened?" the doc asked, his hands still moving. Probing. "Hockey? Skiing?"

Zack sucked in a sharp breath as pain shafted to his knee. *Get it over with, buddy—cut out the small talk.* "I fell—" he stared at the man in the white coat, daring him to so much as chuckle "—off a kitchen chair."

Not so much as a twinkle brightened the doctor's impassive expression. He shook his head. "It never ceases to amaze me, the number of people who—"

"Jeez!"

"That hurt?" The doctor's voice was impersonal.

Of course it damned well hurt! "Yeah, you could say so."

"Right." The doctor wrote something on a chart.

"We'll get the ankle X-rayed." He turned and crossed with brisk steps to the nurses' station.

Zack stared dismally at the ceiling. What lousy timing! Of all the days for him to end up here, just when it was so incredibly important for him to be somewhere else.

He raked a distraught hand through his hair as he thought of Arabella, pictured her arriving at the airport.

From what he remembered of her, she'd been a sweet little kid. Funny, bright, lovable. But now she must be lost and lonely and desperately needing comfort, just as he had been after Becky had died. As he still was.

He closed his eyes as the old familiar pain swamped him. But he rode with it, as he'd finally learned to do.

In the beginning, he'd made it harder for himself. He'd fought the pain in those darkest of dark days, when his loss was fresh and each waking hour a hell to be endured. Everybody knew that men were supposed to be strong, and he'd wanted to be strong for Lauren. He'd blocked out his own suffering so he could comfort her in hers.

But she'd wanted no comfort from him.

And it wasn't till after she left their marriage that he opened himself to his agony. Alone, he'd ranted and raged at the cruel God who had taken his child. And then had come the parties. He'd thrown himself frantically at life, as if a surfeit of activity could somehow cancel out his sorrow. It hadn't worked, he admitted that. And added to his sorrow was anger. Anger at Lauren, for not letting him comfort her in her grief. And anger at her for not comforting him in his.

Today he'd had to delegate his wife to go to the airport in his place. He'd had no option. But if Arabella

reached out to Lauren for comfort, would Lauren take
the child into her heart?

Or would she, bound up in her own grief as she was,
reject Arabella in exactly the same way she had rejected
him?

"Mr. and Mrs. Zack Alexander, please report to the pub-
lic meet and greet area on level two. Repeat, Mr. and
Mrs. Zack Alexander to the meet and greet area on level
two..."

Laura had been hovering at Gate E79, where passen-
gers from Arabella's flight had been filtering through in
small groups. She heard the announcement and hurried
to the meet and greet area.

There she was directed to a uniformed airline em-
ployee.

"Ah, Mrs. Alexander. You've come to collect
Arabella Smith?"

"That's right."

"May I see your ID, please?"

"Of course." Lauren handed over her driver's licence.

The woman scrutinized the photograph and compared
it at some length with the reality before handing it back.

"Thank you. Now if you would just sign this release
form..."

When Lauren had completed it, the woman said,

"I'm afraid Arabella was quite sick on the flight.
Nerves, probably. Flying alone at that age can be pretty
scary. She's feeling a bit better now, though. Shall we
go and see if—" She broke off as she glanced over
Lauren's shoulder. "Ah, here she is."

Take it easy, Lauren told herself. *You can handle this.
You can.*

She turned and had the strange feeling the rest of the world had been put on hold as she saw two people approaching from the crowd, a flight attendant and a child.

Arabella was taller than she'd expected, skinnier than she'd remembered, and the carroty red hair had mellowed to a glorious auburn. She was wearing an emerald jacket, blue jeans and a backpack, and the soles of her high tops squeaked on the tiled floor as she walked. When she came to a halt a few feet from Lauren, Lauren saw that her face was so white her freckles stood out like a sprinkling of finely grated dark chocolate. And her eyelids were flickering, her eyes shadowed with nervousness.

Poor kid, Lauren thought, *she looks terrified.*

"Hi, Arabella," she said softly.

With a faltering smile, Arabella took a squeaky step forward, drew her hands out of her pockets, started to raise her arms as if for a welcoming hug—

Lauren froze. Just as she did in her nightmares when she tried to run and her feet wouldn't move. She froze. *Reach out,* a voice cried from the depths of her soul. *Reach out....*

At last the power surged into her limbs. But she saw with a gut-wrenching stab of guilt that it was too late. She had hesitated too long. The moment was gone, the moment was lost. Arabella hadn't stepped back, but she had withdrawn emotionally. Her eyes were shuttered. And she was clutching the straps of her backpack, her knuckles white, her bony elbows pointed straight at Lauren.

Blocking her off.

"Arabella—"

"Hi, Aunt Lauren." The child's voice was taut. "Thanks for coming to meet me."

On the drive from the airport, Arabella made no attempt to open conversation. Lauren searched her mind for topics of interest but could think of nothing to say that would break the ice. She couldn't ask about the child's mother or father, didn't want to ask about Dolly Smith. In the end, she decided it might be safe to ask about school.

Arabella shrugged. "It's okay," she said, staring out the window. "And if I don't like it here, the principal told me I could come back and spend the Christmas holidays with her and three other girls who'll be spending their vacation there because their parents are abroad."

She made it sound as if she didn't give a hoot where she'd be for Christmas, but Lauren sensed it was a front.

"Your uncle Zack's looking forward to having you for the next couple of weeks," she murmured as she wheeled the Mercedes off South Granville and onto her own street. "I'm sure you'll have a good time with him."

Out of the corner of her eye, she saw the child jerk her head round. "You mean," Arabella said, "you're not going to be there?"

"No. Your uncle Zack and I...well, we're not really married any more. We don't live together. I have a condo up there—" Lauren gestured toward her building "—and he lives at Lindenlea, our old house in Point Grey."

"How come Uncle Zack got the house and you just got a condo?"

"I was the one who...walked out of our marriage. Besides, I didn't want the house." *Too many memories.*

"Do you live alone?"

"Yes."

"Do you have a boyfriend?"

"No."

"Does Uncle Zack live alone?"

I'm not sure, though I've tortured myself often enough, wondering. "You'll have to ask him about that."

"Where is he? Why didn't he meet me?"

"He broke his ankle this morning. He's at the hospital having it fixed. He's going to phone me when he's discharged, and I'll drive you over to his place."

"I remember Uncle Zack," Arabella said wistfully. "He was lots of fun."

Lauren swung the car into the parking lot. "Yes." The word caught in her throat. "He was. Lots of fun."

Zack didn't phone till quite late that evening.

"Where on earth are you?" Lauren asked.

"Still at the hospital. Did you get Arabella?"

"Yes, she's here. She was sick on the plane, but she's feeling better. She's watching TV at the moment. When can I pick you up?"

"Change of plan, I'm afraid. Doc's keeping me in overnight. When I fell—"

"You never did tell me what happened. Fell where?"

"Er, off a chair. In, er, the sitting room. And I cracked my head on the edge of the coffee table on my way down." He spoke quickly as if he didn't want to discuss it. "At any rate, seems I've got a slight concussion, and the doc wants to keep an eye on me. All being well, I'll get out in the morning.''

"So that means—''

"You'll have Arabella tonight.''

"Zack, that was not the deal. It's out of the question—''

A small sound behind her made her turn. Arabella was standing in the doorway. Her face looked pale and pinched.

"Lauren?'' Zack's voice seemed to be coming from far away. "You still there?''

"Yes.'' Keeping her gaze steadily on Arabella, she bit back the words of protest that had risen to her lips. "That's fine. Just call me in the morning—and let's hope you're better by then.''

"Thanks, Lauren. I owe you one.''

"More than one, Zack,'' she said silkily, and hung up.

Arabella's right thumb had found its way into her mouth. "I'm to stay here tonight?'' she asked around it.

"That's right.'' Lauren managed a reassuring smile.

"But where am I to sleep? You only have one bedroom.''

"There's a bed in the den. You'll have the room all to yourself, and I believe the bed's quite comfy.''

Arabella yawned. "I think I'll go to bed now. Is it okay to have a bath first? I feel yukky after being sick.''

'No problem. Need any help?'' she asked, as they went into the hall, where Arabella's luggage still stood.

"Oh, no.'' Arabella hefted the smaller of her two cases. "I'm very self-sufficient. That's one of the things they teach us at the Sheldon School for Girls.''

Arabella came into the den as Lauren finished making the bed. She looked pretty and feminine in an ankle-length white cotton nightie with a pattern of dainty lemon roses on the yoke.

"I scrubbed the bath when I was finished, Aunt Lauren." She folded her clothes and placed them in a neat pile on the armchair by the hearth.

"Did you remember to clean your teeth?" Lauren asked automatically.

Arabella walked to her and held up her face, lips drawn back, pearly teeth gritted together, gaze expectant.

Lauren was slammed by an image of Becky in that same pose, her eyes dancing as she waited for praise.

"Lovely!" Lauren's voice came out huskily. "Whiter than white." She pulled back the duvet. "Hop in."

Arabella scrambled into bed, and Lauren tucked the duvet under her chin. She reached for the light on the end table, but paused when Arabella spoke.

"I don't suppose..."

"Mmm?"

Arabella curled her fingers around the duvet. She shook her head. "It was nothing, Aunt Lauren. Good night."

Lauren hesitated for a second, but Arabella had already closed her eyes.

"Good night, Arabella." She leaned over and brushed a kiss on the child's brow, her heart aching as the clean soap scent and silk-smooth texture of her skin disturbed painfully poignant memories. "Sweet dreams."

When she left the den, she closed the door quietly behind her, then slumped against the wall.

It wasn't fair. It wasn't fair that Zack had broken his ankle, wasn't fair that he was stuck in hospital, wasn't fair she was forced to endure this heart-wrenching pain of having a child in her life again.

But it was only for one night.

And not even that, really. Arabella would be in the den. She, Lauren, would be in her bedroom. At most she'd have to spend maybe another couple of hours with her in the morning, while they waited for Zack to get the all clear.

A couple more hours. She could surely cope with that.

A small sound awoke her in the middle of the night.

She was lying on her stomach, her head to one side on the pillow, her face toward the door. She froze. Pulses racing. Ears strained.

And heard the door creak open.

She stared in horror, not daring to breathe. Her curtains were closed but they were of pale silk and allowed a thin light to filter into the room. She heard another creak, and her heart stopped. A hundred dread scenarios leaped into her brain, each one more horrific than the last. She got ready to scream.

In the shadowy dark she saw a figure creep toward her.

A small figure.

In a white nightie.

Arabella.

She sagged with relief, almost laughed aloud at her fanciful fears. But what could the child want? Was she perhaps feeling sick again?

About to ask the question, Lauren caught the words when she felt the corner of her duvet being lifted. Next, she felt the mattress dip, so slightly she'd not have noticed it had she been asleep. Then a warm body snuggled against her, a wiry arm slipped around her waist, two small feet tucked their way into the folds of her satin nightie, ten bony toes wriggled against her calves.

She heard a contented sigh, and within thirty seconds Arabella's light breathing had become deep and rhythmic, and Lauren knew the child had already gone back to sleep.

Next morning, when Lauren awoke, she was alone.

And if there hadn't been a long, shiny strand of bright auburn hair on the white pillow next her own, she might have been tempted to believe the whole episode had been a dream.

Zack phoned at nine-thirty.

"I've got the all clear," he said. "I'm just going to call a cab and I'll be on my way. See you in about—"

"Forget the cab. Be at the main entrance in ten minutes. I'll pick you up and take you straight home."

"No, I don't want—"

Lauren hung up. No way was she going to have him coming to her place. The man had an uncanny knack of getting his own way. Once in here, she'd never get rid of him. And she had to get the message across, once and for all, that whatever they had in the past was over.

She had to convince him of that.

Not for her sake, but for his own.

CHAPTER THREE

Damn crutches!

Zack shot them into the back seat of the white Mercedes and followed them clumsily.

"Thanks for the drive," he said to Lauren as he levered his injured leg onto the dove gray leather seat.

"No problem." She glanced in her side mirror before pulling away from the curb.

"Hey, Arabella!" He grinned at the little girl who had twisted around so she could sneak a look at him from between the two front seats. "How's it going?"

"Fine, thank you." Her green eyes were wary, but when he thrust his hand out she poked hers forward between the seats and allowed him to shake it. It was, of course, lost in his, but he was surprised by the strength in her fingers.

"Great to see you!" he said.

"You too, Uncle Zack." She slid her hand free and faced front again.

Zack slouched back, drained by the effort of appearing cheerful. Not only did his ankle hurt like hell, this whole situation had the makings of disaster. Lauren would blow her top if she saw the state of the sitting room... and with good reason.

He suppressed a despairing groan. At all costs, he had to keep her from getting even a glimpse of the interior of the house, the house that had once been a home and now was just a building with walls and a roof and appliances and furniture. What was missing was...heart.

He found the thought so depressing he couldn't work up the energy to initiate further conversation, but when they were almost home he roused himself from his stupor.

"Would you mind swinging by that London Drugs on the corner?" he asked. "I need to get a prescription filled."

"Sure."

Lauren pulled into the busy parking lot, and after circling a couple of times, eventually was lucky enough to find a spot. She switched off the engine, turned.

"I'll get it," she said, holding out her hand.

"Thanks. It'd be quicker."

After she'd gone, Arabella opened her seat belt, scrambled to a kneeling position facing backward, grasped the top of her seat and peeked at him.

"Uncle Zack, you're not really my uncle, are you?"

"No, honey, I'm what's called an honorary uncle, just as Lauren's your honorary aunt. Actually, I think it's better than being a real uncle or aunt, because it means you were chosen, instead of just being stuck with each other."

She sighed. "Like Great-Aunt Dolly Smith."

He hid a wry smile and decided it would not be politic to discuss the old bitch. "Your dad and I grew up together, you know, best buddies, and then we both got married around the same time. Your mom and Lauren got to be friends, too."

"My mom and dad were really upset that you didn't want to visit any more...after Becky died."

"Yeah, honey." Zack would have given anything to

put the clock back, but it could never happen. Hadn't he picked up the phone a hundred times, though, in the weeks after Becky's death? Aching with the need to talk to his old friend, to spill out what was in his heart. But then he'd picture the three of them—Mac and Lisa…and Arabella—and he'd always drawn his hand from the phone, knowing if he heard Arabella in the background he'd break down. Later, after Lauren walked out of their marriage, he deliberately cut himself off from most of the couples they'd socialized with. Major mistake. And what he'd missed because of it! Now it was too late. "We lost touch," he said, his voice rough with emotion.

"Because you were feeling sad." Arabella's eyes told him she knew that feeling only too well.

For a few long seconds conversation lapsed, and then she said, "Uncle Zack, do you live alone?"

"Yeah, I live alone."

"Aunt Lauren said you're split up. Does that mean I'm staying with you? Forever?"

His heart twisted with compassion when he saw the anxiety and vulnerability in her eyes. "Honey, if that's what you want. But you don't have to commit yourself yet."

"Do you want me to stay?"

"Yeah, I want you to stay. I think it'll take a bit of adjusting on both our parts, but I'm sure we can make it work."

"Will I have to go back to boarding school?"

He sensed she was holding her breath. "Don't you like it there?"

"It's better than being at Great-Aunt Dolly Smith's, that's for sure." She disappeared from sight, and a second later, he heard the click of her seat belt. "But it's not like being in a family.'' Her voice was muffled. ''It's not like being in a family at all.''

Lauren shivered as she returned to the car, not so much from the biting wind as from anxiety about Zack. He looked awful. Drawn and tense, eyes strained. As he'd made his way from the hospital's entranceway to the car, he'd seemed groggy, and she'd half-expected him to fall flat on his face.

Was he in a fit state to look after a child?

She thought not.

She wondered if he had a housekeeper. Yes, he probably did. He'd never be able to keep their enormous Point Grey house tidy—far less clean—on his own.

With a deliberate effort, she brushed aside her doubts. He'd manage fine. And if he didn't...well, he wasn't her problem. And never would be again.

''Ooh, Christmas lights! That's so pretty, Uncle Zack!'' Eyes wide, Arabella stared at the red and green lights tastefully adorning the beautiful Georgian-style house as Lauren drove the Mercedes up the circular driveway. ''Aunt Lauren doesn't have any Christmas decorations up.''

Lauren felt her stomach muscles clench. She hadn't celebrated Christmas—or any other festive event—during the past four years. ''That's because I plan to be out of town for the next couple of weeks.'' She pulled the car to a halt in front of the house. ''I'm going on a holiday. The day after tomorrow.''

''You didn't tell me that!'' Zack's voice was accusing. ''Where are you going?''

''Toronto.''

"Toronto? Why not Hawaii, the Caribbean, Bermuda, somewhere warm and relaxing? Good grief, Toronto in winter's not the place for a vacation!"

"It's not just a vacation." She met his gaze in the rearview mirror. "I'll be looking for a condo because I'm going to be moving there. I've been offered a promotion. I'll be managing the Ontario end of the business. It's a plum posting, Zack. I consider myself very lucky to get it."

His eyes had a stunned expression that made her feel like an absolute heel. She jerked her gaze away and turned to Arabella, then leaned over and opened her door.

"Well, this is it, Arabella. I hope things go really well with you and your uncle Zack."

"Thanks, Aunt Lauren." The child got out, dragging her backpack. She slammed the door shut, then turned, rounded the car and knocked on Lauren's window.

Lauren slid it down. "What is it, dear?"

Arabella bit her lip. "I...snuck into your bed last night," she said in a low voice. "I just wanted you to know. I was...lonely. I was missing my mom."

Lauren felt as if someone had tied a wire around her neck and was strangling her. She wanted to speak, knew that if she tried, she'd burst into tears.

Arabella walked toward the house. Her thin shoulders were hunched. Lauren thought she'd never seen such a forlorn figure in her life.

She closed her window, hardly able to see for the blurring of her eyes.

She waited for Zack's explosive oath, cringed inside as she waited for him to tell her what an awful person she was.

All she heard was a sigh and then the door opening, the crunch of cases on the gravel as he shoved Arabella's baggage out—one small case, one large, then the clatter of crutches, followed by the sound of the door being closed, firmly but without anger.

Lauren could barely see for the surging tears. She gripped the steering wheel tightly, switched on the ignition, thought she'd never felt more miserable.

Through her tears, she saw Zack wobbling beside Arabella's cases. He was looking at them with a bewildered expression, obviously wondering how the dickens he was going to get them inside. She had never used crutches. She could only imagine how frustrating it must be to be unable to do things you normally took for granted.

"Oh, darn it!" she muttered, blinking away her tears.

She switched off the ignition, opened the door, got out and grabbed a case in each hand.

"I'll carry these inside," she said, "before I go."

"No!" His protest rang with dismay. "No, I can manage!"

"And elephants can fly!"

She strode away from him and made for the front door. She heard him hopping after her. When she got there, she stood with Arabella waiting for him to unlock it. He was taking his own sweet time.

Why had he sounded so dismayed by her offer to help? Was it some macho male thing? Or was there more to it?

At last he opened the door. "Right," he said, "I'll take it from here."

Why so reluctant to have her come inside? Till now, he'd been making every effort to get her back into his life. Now he didn't want her to come into his house. She walked past him and into the foyer.

"Where do you want the cases?" she asked, her gaze flicking briskly around. "I guess upstairs—"

She gasped as she looked into the sitting room.

For a moment, she could only stare, aghast.

Then she dropped the cases and walked like a robot to the open doorway. Her appalled gaze acknowledged and dismissed the overturned chair, the bucket of water. It swiftly moved to skim the revolting pizza stain on the wall, the dirty glasses and plates on every flat surface, the foul-smelling overflowing ashtrays.

And finally, it settled on the skimpy black bra that lay in a snaky slither on the off-white carpet.

She felt the hair at her nape rise in horror and outrage. A photograph of the scene would not have been out of place on the cover of some sleazy tabloid.

And this was the kind of environment to which she was surrendering Arabella?

She spun around.

Zack was right behind her, a sheepish grin on his face. The grin made her see red. But somehow she managed, because of Arabella, to control herself.

"Get on the phone, Zack," she said with fake pleasantry, and had the grim satisfaction of seeing him wince. "Call in a cleaning company. I'll get Arabella settled upstairs, and then you and I are going to have a little talk."

Zack stood at the hall table with the Yellow Pages open in front of him and called every cleaning company listed till he found a dispatcher who would listen to him.

"Today?" the woman echoed with a hysterical laugh.

"The week before Christmas? Mister, don't you know that everybody and their aunt wants their houses cleaned this time of year? Why don't you check the Yellow Pages, try—"

"I've tried them all," he said wearily. "A to Z. You're my last hope. For Pete's sake, it's only one room! How long could that take?"

Silence. Then, "Only one room?"

"Yeah, just one. Look." He pulled out all the stops. "I've just inherited a kid—an eight-year-old orphan— and I need the place nice for her, for the holidays."

"What street are you on?" Her voice had softened.

He gave her the street name and held his breath.

"Okay, mister, this is your lucky day. But sight unseen, that room's gonna cost you big bucks. How does this sound?"

He rolled his eyes at the price she quoted but said without a quaver, "Fine."

"Miriam's on your block. I'll page her, have her pop around to your place on the way to her next client."

He heaved a fervent sigh of relief as he put down the phone.

Perhaps he could get into Lauren's good books again if he had a cup of coffee waiting for her when she came downstairs. Hot coffee, black and very strong. That was how she took it. How she'd always taken it.

Yeah, he thought with a wolfish smile as he retrieved his crutches from their resting place against the wall, and hobbled toward the kitchen. Things were looking up.

"This was the bedroom where you slept last time you visited, Arabella." Lauren set the child's cases down and tried in vain to fight the bittersweet memories triggered by the familiar surroundings. "Do you remember it?"

Arabella looked around the airy room with its blue walls, white wicker furniture, blue and white curtains and duvet. "Yes, I remember. It was right next to Becky's. Becky's bedroom was pink. Is it still pink?"

"No." Lauren crossed to the window and looked into the winter-bare backyard with its trellised gazebo and covered-up swimming pool. "After we moved all Becky's things out, we had the walls painted." She shrugged. "I can't remember what color. Stone, I think."

Lifeless and gray, the way she'd felt. That had been just after the frenzy that had seized her six months after Becky's death. She'd made a phone call to the Salvation Army, told them she wanted to donate a room of furniture, toys, clothes.

She'd watched with blank eyes as the huge truck had come and two men had taken everything away. She had hardly heard Zack's voice pleading with her not to act so hastily, not while she was so distraught.

And later, after she'd had the pink carpet ripped out, she'd phoned Desmond's Painting Company and someone had come and painted the walls. Stone. Yes, it *had* been stone.

Had Zack had it repainted after she left?

'I'm going to put my things away, Aunt Lauren."

She blinked and looked around. Arabella had opened both her cases and was setting jumbled piles of paperbacks and Barbies and Barbie accoutrements on the duvet.

"You'll come down when you're finished?" Lauren asked.

"Yup, I will."

Lauren went into the corridor.

She started toward the landing, but as she passed Becky's room, she came to an abrupt halt. The last thing in the world she wanted to do was look inside the room, but a relentless compulsion drove her to reach for the doorknob.

Bracing herself, she turned the handle and pushed the door open.

The room was empty. And it was exactly as she'd left it. Rose pink carpet gone. Oak floor exposed. Walls the color of stone. Small-paned windows bare of curtains.

She leaned limply against the doorjamb, swamped by the images that superimposed themselves on the empty room. Lost herself in those images. And lost all sense of time.

It was with a heart-juddering shock, as if she'd been called back from a traumatic journey into outer space, that she suddenly heard the clangor of the door bell.

Jerking upright, she stepped into the corridor and closed the door behind her. When she reached the landing, she looked down, but there was no sign of Zack.

The bell rang again.

Could it be the cleaners? How fortunate if he'd managed to get someone to come so quickly at this busy time of year.

She ran down the stairs. In the foyer she paused. She thought she heard noises in the kitchen.

"I'll get it!" she called.

And made for the front door.

When she opened it, it was to find a striking brunette posing seductively on the stoop, her chocolate-brown hair falling sleekly around her padded shoulders. She

was wearing a faux mink coat, and when she saw
Lauren, her lips curved in an equally faux smile.

Certainly not a Jiffy Maid! Lauren thought cynically.
But then, who?

"May I help you?" Lauren said.

"I'm looking for Zack."

"Oh. Come in, then. He's around somewhere."

The woman pranced in on her four-inch heels, bringing with her an almost visible haze of some exotic perfume. Brushing back the faux mink, she revealed a
slinky metallic minidress, a pair of endlessly long legs
encased in the sheerest of pewter nylons and a pair of
perfect knees.

Her gaze flicked over Lauren's classic cream shirt and
tailored slacks. "You must be the housekeeper," she
said dismissively. She looked around. "Would you fetch
Zack?"

Lauren was about to explain haughtily that she was
most certainly not the housekeeper when she heard the
rhythmic hit-thump of crutches and foot on the parquet
floor of the corridor leading from the kitchen.

"Mr. Alexander," she called in her sweetest voice,
"you have a visitor."

Mr. Alexander?

Zack frowned. Why so formal all of a sudden? He
was struck by an awful feeling of foreboding. Whatever
was going on, a cup of hot coffee wasn't going to let
him off the hook.

"Miriam from ZipZap Cleaners?" he called. But
when he hopped into the foyer, he cursed silently and
said brightly, "Ah, no, not Miriam from ZipZap

Cleaners. Hi, there—'' he wracked his befuddled brains and avoided looking at Lauren ''—Alyssia?''

Alyssia smiled, all white teeth and curving fuchsia lips. ''Zack, sweetie, when I got home from your party the other night I discovered I'd left something here!''

He raised his brows. ''Left something?'' Beyond her, he could see Lauren turning away, and he was gratified that she was understanding enough to leave them alone. Decent of her, he thought as she disappeared into the sitting room, to give them some privacy.

''So.'' He moved forward. ''Alyssia, what was it you left?''

She parted her lips to speak, but before she could, Lauren appeared behind her and tapped her on the shoulder.

The ankle-length hem of Alyssia's fur coat swung out as she swiveled on her dangerously high heels.

''Is this what you're looking for?'' Lauren asked. She was, Zack saw, holding out something black and flimsy and—

He gulped and wished the floor would yawn open and let him sink to oblivion. *He* wasn't the one who had removed the woman's bra. But expect Lauren to believe that? Nah!

Lauren's smile was innocent, her eyes guileless. ''Let's just check the label of this strapless little beauty and make sure it's yours,'' she went on in a silky tone. ''Let's see now. It's...oh—'' fake awe ''—Frederick's of Hollywood! And oh, my gosh! it's a size thirty-six triple D!''

Alyssia thrust out her breasts and fluttered her mascaraed lashes. ''Impressed, huh? Most people are.''

Lauren firmly grasped her arm and frog marched her to the front door.

"Hey, hang on," the brunette protested. "What are you doing! I came here to see Zack—"

"Well, you've seen him." Lauren slung the bra around the woman's neck. "So now you can go."

"Sugar lumps," Alyssia whined at Zack over Lauren's shoulder, "can't you stop her? What kind of a housekeeper is she, anyway, to treat your guests this way?"

"I'm not his housekeeper," Lauren snapped as she maneuvered the brunette out. She added venomously as she slammed the door in her outraged face, "I'm his *wife!*"

If Arabella hadn't chosen that precise moment to come downstairs, Zack wondered what might have happened next. Would Lauren have flayed him alive for his choice of company? Yeah, he was pretty sure that's what would have happened.

But even as she turned, two spots of scarlet flagging her cheeks, he found himself wondering why she'd gotten so worked up over Alyssia. Why should it bother her? She was the one who had walked out on the marriage. She was the one who had told him to make a new life for himself. Was it possible her anger had been caused by jealousy?

The possibility flamed another spark of hope and made him scrutinize her carefully as she spoke to Arabella.

"Finished unpacking?" she said as the child ran down the last few steps of the staircase.

"Yup. Who was that?"

The tightening of her lips was the only visible sign of her distaste. "A friend of your uncle Zack's."

"I was watching from the landing." Arabella's eyes twinkled. "I thought it was Cruella de Vil!"

Lauren chuckled, so he chuckled, too. But when her gaze sliced to him, he realized her laughter had been superficial, and the hard, contemptuous look she aimed at him was sharp as the point of a knife.

Ouch!

"Her name's Alyssia, dear." Lauren's voice was pleasant as she addressed Arabella. "Isn't that a *pretty* name? Your uncle Zack has lots of friends, and if they're all as...interesting...as Alyssia, it's no wonder he's got a reputation for throwing really fun parties!"

He was sure the child wouldn't detect the sarcasm in Lauren's tone. He pretended he didn't notice it, either.

"I've made coffee," he said, turning a bland gaze her way. "Let's go to the kitchen—"

The doorbell rang.

This time it was Miriam from ZipZap Cleaners.

As he ushered her in, he saw Lauren and Arabella take off in the direction of the kitchen. He showed the cleaner into the sitting room, gave her instructions, then left her to get on with it.

When he entered the kitchen, it was to find Lauren alone, looking into the fridge.

"Where's Arabella?" he asked.

"She went upstairs to fetch a book. Zack," she said irritably, "there's nothing in here."

He hopped across the kitchen and peered over her shoulder. "There's beer," he said, "and there's white wine, and there's cheese and some, er, nibbly things... from the last party—"

He reared back as she swung the door shut.

Her expression was grim as she faced him, her hands rammed onto her hips.

"I'll go out and get groceries." Her tone was as grim as her expression. "Enough to keep you and Arabella going for the next several days. But Zack, you're going to have to smarten up if you plan on keeping Arabella—"

The phone rang.

He grasped at the opportunity to escape her searing disapproval.

He hopped over and grabbed the receiver. "Alexander."

"Ah, Mr. Alexander, this is Tyler Braddock."

"Mr. Braddock." He looked at Lauren, raised his brows. She met his questioning stare coldly. "What can I do for you?"

He listened, and as he did, he wanted to swear. He nodded, kept his gaze locked with Lauren's, said, "Yes, I understand," at regular intervals, and finally, "Right, Mr. Braddock, yes, I can see it's a problem, but I'll work on it and get back to you ASAP."

He hung up.

"What?" Lauren stepped forward, frowning. "What's wrong?" She had a sinking feeling that whatever it was, it was bad. Really bad.

Her breath caught in her throat as she watched Zack lean heavily against the wall.

"What's wrong," he said, "is that Arabella's great-aunt Dolly Smith has found out that you and I are estranged, and she's claiming this invalidates Mac and Lisa's will. She wants Arabella back. She says it's her duty to bring the girl up and she's going to sue for custody.''

''But the woman must be eighty!''

''Sixty-five and healthy as a horse, and still has all her faculties!''

''Oh, Zack!'' Lauren put a hand on the table to steady herself. ''You can't let her have Arabella. That little girl needs someone who loves her and *wants* to care for her, not someone driven by a sense of duty!''

''Of course she does—but that's not the way a judge is going to see it. Given a choice between placing the child with a relative, one who's conscientious and upright, and a woman, to boot—or placing her with someone who's not related, someone who's known around town for his wild parties, and a man, to boot...'' Zack rubbed a hand tiredly around his nape. ''Lauren, I don't have a hope in hell of winning the case.''

''Uncle Zack?''

With a feeling of dismay, Lauren swung her attention to the doorway where Arabella stood, *Goosebumps* paperback in hand, abject misery on her face.

How long had she been there?

''Honey,'' Zack said, but Arabella broke in.

''I heard what you were saying about Great-Aunt Dolly Smith. She wants me back.'' She blinked, and he knew she was bravely fighting tears. ''And I'm gonna have to go, right?''

Zack's eyes had a bleak expression, and Lauren could guess what he was thinking. He'd feel as if he were letting Arabella down.

But he had done his best. He'd been prepared to welcome Arabella into his life while she, Lauren, had—

Arabella gave a great gulping sob and took off along

the corridor. From the kitchen, Lauren heard her footsteps as she ran helter-skelter up the stairs.

Zack pushed himself from the wall and started after
her.

Lauren stood frozen. She'd never felt so mixed up.
She couldn't bear the thought of Great-Aunt Dolly Smith
having permanent charge of Arabella. And she knew that
if she didn't offer to help, that would happen.

But if she did help out, it would mean the loss of her
promotion. And it would mean moving in with Zack.

But down the road other promotions would come her
way. And moving in with Zack needn't be permanent.
It need only be till the custody case was over. And perhaps a little longer. Till Arabella was securely settled.
Till she, Lauren, was convinced Zack had cleaned up his
act. Then she could move out again and leave him to
bring up Arabella alone.

If she was very careful, she could avoid becoming
emotionally involved with Arabella. If she was very
careful, she could avoid taking the child into her heart.

It could be done.

And she would do it.

She took a deep breath as she made her decision.

She could hear Zack's crutches and foot hitting the
parquet floor in the corridor at a rate of knots.

Feeling as if she were hyperventilating, she hurried
after him.

She caught up with him at the foot of the stairs.

She grabbed his shirt sleeve, and he turned, frowning.

''I'll come home,'' she said breathlessly. ''But it'll
only be till you get legal custody of Arabella. Nothing

has changed between us, Zack,'' she added quickly as she saw the flare of hope in his eyes. "It'll be separate bedrooms, separate lives. Together in name only. Do we have a deal?''

CHAPTER FOUR

"NO, LAUREN, we do not have a deal."

Zack's adamant voice echoed in Lauren's head half an hour later as she wrestled an obstinate-wheeled metal cart along the busy aisles of the nearest Safeway. His refusal had stunned her.

"Why on earth not?" she'd said, staring.

He'd leaned against the newel post and met her bewildered gaze with a look of disapproval...or it might have been disappointment.

"In the first place," he said, "it would be a lie."

"Surely in this case the end would justify the means?"

"Because Arabella would become my ward, rather than her great-aunt Dolly Smith's?"

"Yes!"

"Okay, but what lesson do you think that kind of manipulation would teach the child? Furthermore—"

At the memory of the way his upper lip had curled as he'd said the word *manipulation,* Lauren felt her cheeks become hot. Scowling, she snatched a giant cereal package from a shelf and tossed it on top of a bulk pack of canned tomato soup.

"Furthermore—" his eyes had become shuttered "—if I did win the case, how do you think Arabella would feel, seeing you walk away as soon as the dust had settled? *Devastated,* that's how she would feel! Lauren, the kid desperately needs a mother. She's fond of you already, and she's ripe for becoming even more emotionally involved. I'm not about to create a family and then pull the rug from under her feet. Arabella needs stability and security, and *that's* what I aim to give her." He added in a gentler tone, "I know you made the offer with the best of intentions, but sometimes good intentions aren't enough."

With that, he'd turned, grabbed the banister and clumsily started hopping up the stairs.

"What are you going to *do,* then?" she called after him.

"I guess I'll have to find me a nanny," he said over his shoulder.

A nanny.

Lauren rounded the aisle and maneuvered the recalcitrant cart to the checkout. Yes, she thought, a nanny would be the answer. A nanny who was warm and affectionate and met life head-on, not someone like herself, whose life was beset by panic and fear.

The panic and fear that had made her reject Zack.

The panic and fear that made her say no to love.

"I feel so damned useless," Zack grumbled as he watched Lauren unload bulging brown paper bags onto the kitchen table. Her cheeks were pink, the color whipped there by the wintry wind, and her cobalt toque was spattered with snowflakes. "Give me something to do, for Pete's sake!"

"Why don't you sit down and write out a job description for the nanny you're going to hire." She slid a half-gallon jug of skim milk onto the bottom shelf of the fridge.

"I've already called a top agency—they're going to

start sending me candidates for interviewing at the beginning of the week. The woman I talked to said she had five or six possibles on her books." He sat at the table and stretched out his injured leg, making sure to keep it and his crutches out of Lauren's path.

"Sounds promising." She scooped up a ten-pound bag of sugar and carried it to the cupboard. "Have you told Arabella what you're planning?"

"Yeah, we talked in her room when you were out." As Lauren reached up, his gaze was drawn to her breasts, to the sweet curves licked by the clinging silk of her cream blouse. He thought of touching her, remembered how he used to touch her, and with the memories came desire. Desire that fired his blood. Desire he quickly got under control. "She wasn't too keen on the idea. Actually," he amended wryly, "that's putting it mildly."

Lauren raised her eyebrows.

"She threw a tantrum." He grimaced. "She said she was way too old, only babies had nannies and I couldn't make her have one, I wasn't her dad. You should have seen her, hands on her hips, glaring at me—a regular little spitfire!" He didn't tell Lauren that a moment later the child had broken down completely and thrown herself on the bed, sobbing her heart out. ""If Aunt Lauren liked me enough,'" she'd cried, ""she'd want to be my mom and then I wouldn't need any old nanny!'" He'd held her shuddering body in his arms till her sobs had slowed to erratic hiccups, then he'd quietly explained that her aunt Lauren was still missing Becky so much she didn't have room in her heart for anyone else.

"Zack?" Lauren's voice made him start.

"Oh…sorry, my mind wandered there."

"You eventually persuaded Arabella it would be okay to have a nanny?"

"Yeah. She's dead set against going into Dolly's care, and I was able to convince her that having a reliable nanny would go a long way to helping our case in court."

"Well, that's good."

"Then afterward I almost broke my neck coming down the stairs," he said with a dry laugh. "So I've decided to use the main floor bedroom till I get this damned cast off."

"Where will you put the nanny?" She hauled a mesh sack of onions from one of the grocery bags.

"I thought," he said carefully, "in...Becky's room. So she'd be next door to Arabella."

The air in the kitchen stilled. He felt his nape prickle. He waited, nerves taut, to see what she would say.

For a moment, she stood frozen, for all the world like a film on pause on the VCR, and then, as if someone had pressed play, she lifted the onions.

"You'll have to have the room redecorated." Her voice was totally devoid of inflection. "It's...cold-looking, the way it is. Not welcoming."

He clenched his fists and set them on the table. "I expected you'd put up a fight."

Her eyes locked unflinchingly with his. "It's a room, Zack. It's not a shrine. If you want to—"

He winced as a throbbing ache in his ankle sharply intensified. He fumbled for the plastic container of prescription pills in his shirt pocket, flicked off the cap and shook two pills onto his palm.

"I was supposed to have taken these an hour ago," he said. "Could you pass me a glass of water?"

Frowning, Lauren poured the water and he used it to wash down the pills. When he handed back the glass, she said, in a concerned tone, "Are you all right?"

"Oh, yeah, I'm fine."

"You're looking pretty ropey." Her gaze was shrewd. "How are you going to look after Arabella when you're not up to par? You'll have to cook for her and—"

"Don't worry about us, we'll manage. I'll take it easy over the weekend and I'll take next week off and—oh, damn!"

"What now?"

"I have to go in Tuesday and Wednesday...we've got a couple of delegations of Japanese buyers coming for a tour of the plant." He raked his hand through his hair and scowled blackly at the dishwasher as if the answer to his problems might be hidden somewhere inside it.

For a long moment there was silence in the kitchen except for the hum of the fridge. Then he heard Lauren inhale a deep breath.

"Okay. Here's the plan." Her tone was resigned. "I'll cancel my Toronto trip and take over here for the next couple of weeks. At least till you hire a nanny." She tucked the onions away and then turned and looked levelly at him. "You say you feel okay—well, you look like hell. You're going to have enough on your plate just getting around and going to work without worrying about Arabella."

She paused as fast, light steps pattered along the corridor, and then Arabella appeared in the doorway, her face alight with excitement. She was obviously bursting to say something, but she bit her lip when she realized she was interrupting.

"So," Lauren went on, "I'll keep Arabella company during the holidays, on the days you're at the office."

Arabella blinked. "You're not going to Toronto right away?"

"No, I'll be around for a couple of weeks."

"Oh, goody! Aunt Lauren, did you notice it started to snow? Uncle Zack won't be able to go tobogganing, but we can go, right?" Her eyes were bright with hope.

After an almost imperceptible pause, Lauren said, "Sure, we can give it a try if the snow lies. But I'll have to go over to my place and get some jeans and boots."

"You'd better go now," Zack said smoothly, "before the roads get bad. And while you're there," he added, pushing his luck to the max, "why don't you collect some overnight things? I always go into the office early, and I can't leave Arabella alone in the house. I know it's an imposition, but...it'll be handier all around if you sleep here."

Lauren hauled a thick-knit sweater from her closet and added it to the clothes she had packed in her suitcase. She could hardly believe she was doing this!

Zack, she knew, had expected her to turn down his suggestion that she stay. He couldn't have been more surprised than she was when she heard herself say, "Fine."

But really, she reflected defensively as she tossed some underwear on top of her toilet bag, moving in with Zack—for just the two weeks—was the only sensible thing to do. If the snow stayed, it might be hard getting around, especially early in the morning.

So here she was, packing for the holidays...but she

would not, after all, be going to Toronto. She had already canceled her flight.

Before returning to the house, she had quite a few things to do, and when she finally emerged from her building, darkness had fallen.

The roads were treacherously slippery. She saw three fender benders on her way to Point Grey. By the time she reached Lindenlea, her fingers were so tightly gripped around the steering wheel they were almost numb.

The ZipZap Cleaners' van was gone. The lights were on in the sitting room. As she got out of the Mercedes she noticed a small figure appear briefly at the window.

Becky!

For a split second, she thought it was Becky.

Then she was jolted back to reality.

A reality that was cold and harsh and cruel.

She would never see Becky again.

She inhaled shakily, brushed a hand over her eyes, went to the trunk and hauled out her gray case. She slammed the trunk shut and made her way through the snow to the house, head bent against the storm. She was on the stoop, about to use her key, which she had never removed from her key ring, when the door swung open to reveal Arabella.

"Oh, hi, honey." Lauren moved inside. "I see Miriam has gone."

"Mmm. She's gone, but…"

Lauren dropped her case, locked the door, hung up her things. From the sitting room drifted the mingled aroma of bleach and lemon-scented furniture polish.

"Aunt Lauren…"

Lauren frowned as she noticed the strained look in Arabella's eyes.

"What on earth's wrong?"

"Oh, Aunt Lauren you'll never guess what—"

"Ah!" A relieved voice came from her right. "You're back!"

She turned and saw Zack coming out of the sitting room. His eyes were even more strained than Arabella's.

"Has something happened?" she asked.

He raked a hand through his hair, and she felt an ominous sense of foreboding. She knew that gesture, recognized it as a sign of distress.

"Not something," he muttered gloomily. "Somebody!"

"What do you mean, somebody? Who?"

A sound on the landing made her swivel.

At first, she didn't recognize the gaunt figure staring at her from the top of the stairs.

Then the woman put a long hand on the banister, and setting one narrow-booted foot after another with absolute precision, started to descend.

"Great-Aunt Dolly Smith!" Lauren wondered if her heart was going to stop.

The elderly woman paused. The light of the crystal chandelier cast shadows on her face, elongating her thin aristocratic nose, accentuating her high cheekbones, emphasizing the pouches beneath the piercing black eyes.

"Yes, girl." Her voice had a rasping edge, as if rusty with disuse. "It is I."

Frame rigidly erect, she continued down the stairs.

When she reached the bottom she paused again, directly under the chandelier. In its glittering light, her scalp showed pink under sparse silver hair fluffed out in a vain effort to conceal. Her body was all bone and tension, her clothing black. Layer upon layer of it, covering her from her wrinkled white neck to her buttoned black boots.

She looked, Lauren thought, like a picture from a stern Victorian novel. She looked like the kind of woman who put duty before everything else.

Which was, indeed, the kind of woman she was!

"Lauren?"

She blinked as she heard Zack address her.

He cleared his throat. "Great-Aunt Dolly," he informed her, "has just flown up from Los Angeles."

"That's nice." Lauren thought the words were going to choke her but somehow she managed to get them out.

"I've come to see Arabella." Dolly Smith snapped open the chrome buckle of the enormous black patent bag looped over her wrist and whisked out a man's white handkerchief. She blew her nose long and loud, then stuffed the hanky into the bowels of the capacious purse. "It was against my wishes that she travel here alone. Child—" she fixed Arabella with a piercing gaze "—I want to talk to your so-called aunt and uncle. Go up to your room. And we'll have no eavesdropping, do you hear?"

Lauren felt her temper rise at the rude way the woman had addressed Arabella, but even as she opened her mouth to object, Zack gave her a warning poke.

"For God's sake don't antagonize the old witch!" he hissed under his breath. Then, to Arabella, he said, "Honey, would you do something for me before you go up? I've made a pot of tea...it's on the kitchen counter. Set it on a tray, with milk and sugar, and three mugs."

"And cookies? Aunt Lauren bought oatmeal cookies."

"Yeah, that would be great. And could you please bring everything to the sitting room?"

"Sure."

"Thanks, sweetie."

"You're welcome, Uncle Zack."

Arabella skirted her great-aunt as warily as if the woman had been a raging bull and then she broke into a run, her feet making fast sounds on the corridor floor.

"Right," Zack said, "let's the three of us go into the sitting room and have our little chat!"

When Dolly Smith had turned up on his front doorstep, Zack's immediate instinct—after he got over his initial shock—had been to slam the door in her self-righteous face. But he could see that the taillights of her airport cab were already disappearing down the drive.

And her booted toe was already in the door.

"Young man—" she'd shoved an aged brown leather case into his hands "—please take this up to my room. And then I'd like you to make me a pot of tea. Strong tea. Not like the stuff they serve on the airlines these..."

Whatever else she'd said had been drowned out as a powerful gust of wind had shrieked by, blowing her into the entranceway along with a flurry of dry snow.

Suppressing a defeated sigh, Zack had accepted what fate had brought and shut the door.

Well, what else could I have done? he snapped at the inner voice that was mocking him for being such a pushover. *Throw her out? Into the winter storm?*

Hardly!

But now she was in, the question was, how long was she going to stay?

As Lauren ushered her to a comfortable armchair by the hearth, he glanced at the wall beside his Izzard oil. It was spotless. Not a sign left of the uphurled pizza.

Miriam of ZipZap had done an excellent job.

Money well spent.

And the job completed in the nick of time.

What would Dolly Smith's reaction have been had she seen it the way it had been that morning?

He shuddered.

"Zack." Lauren's voice was concerned. "Are you okay?"

He reined in his drifting thoughts. "Oh, er, a bit cold," he fibbed. "I'll...put on the fire."

He hopped over, reached down and flicked the switch by the side of the gas fire. Flames immediately leaped into action, sending out a glow of cozy warmth that supplemented the central heating.

Lauren had taken a seat on one of the chesterfields. He hopped over to join her and set his crutches against the armchair next him.

"So." Dolly's gaze darted fiercely from him to Lauren. "What's the situation? I didn't expect to find *you* here. It was my understanding that you and Zack were estranged. Has the situation changed?"

Zack looked at Lauren. Their eyes met. Hers were clear and steady. He knew, without her having to say so, that her offer was still open. He could tell Dolly Smith the marriage was on again. He had a strong feeling that if he did, if she believed Arabella was going to be brought up in a close and loving family, her resistance to handing over the reins might dissipate.

Dolly was in her mid-sixties. What woman that age really wanted the responsibility of a child, one who in just over four years would be a teenager, with all the problems that entailed?

He hesitated.

Lauren reached over and slipped her hand into his. Reaffirming her support.

He shifted in his seat.

It would be so easy.

He formed the words, opened his mouth—

"Here's the tea, Uncle Zack." Arabella came slowly into the room, holding the tray in front of her with careful hands, keeping her eyes fixed on the stainless steel teapot. "Sorry I was so long, but I spilled some sugar on the floor." For a second her gaze sliced to Lauren. "I could've swept it under the fridge—" her gaze dropped again to the tray "—but I knew that would've been wrong. Mom told me character is how you act even when you know nobody's watching. So I brushed it all up and put it in the garbage."

Zack swallowed the words he'd been about to say.

The lie he'd been sorely tempted to utter.

He watched Arabella set the tray on the coffee table, watched her leave the room after he'd thanked her.

She shut the door behind her.

"So." Dolly Smith sat up straight as a tin soldier. "You're back together again? I have to admit, that makes—"

"No."

She stopped short, jerked her head. Brows down, she glowered at Zack. *'No?''*

"No, Dolly." He felt Lauren's hand quiver in his grasp. "We're not back together. Lauren has kindly of-

fered to move in till I hire a nanny. Possibly she'll be
here for a couple of weeks. After that, she's moving to
Toronto. She's had an offer of a promotion, and she's
accepted it."

He could see he'd taken the old bat by surprise. For
once, she appeared at a loss for words. Her eyes were
more glittering, more penetrating than ever as she scrutinized the pair of them. When finally she spoke, it was
to Lauren.

"Well, girl, don't just sit there like a lump on a log!
Pour the tea!"

Lauren slid the chicken and mushroom casserole out of
the oven and placed it on the butcher block surface of
the island in the middle of the kitchen. As she tilted the
casserole lid, steam belched out, along with the scents
of sweet marjoram, bay leaf and thyme.

She inhaled the tantalizing aroma and savored it. She
hadn't made this recipe in years. It wouldn't have been
economical to cook such a large amount for just one
person. And the last time she had made it, she had been
in this very kitchen.

As she took three wineglasses from the cupboard, she
thought how strange it felt to be working in her own
kitchen again. It was like stepping back in time. Nothing
had changed. Same old pots and pans, same old stove,
same old table, same old cutlery—

She heard the sound of Zack's crutches in the corridor,
and her body tensed. She stood, bracing herself with her
palms on the island, and watched the door.

He appeared, flashed her a smile and headed for the
fridge.

"We'll have wine with dinner." He hauled out a bottle of Pinot Blanc. "Ah—great minds. I see you have wineglasses out already. Pass me the corkscrew?"

The corkscrew was in the right-hand partition in the cutlery drawer, exactly where she'd always kept it. She handed it over and withdrew her hand quickly.

She was nervous around him. And reluctantly aware of the physical attraction that invariably tugged between them when they were together.

"Shall I open a can of soup?" she asked, sliding her hands into her apron pockets.

"What else is there?" he asked, as he propped his crutches against the table behind him.

She gestured toward the casserole. "That, with rice and asparagus."

"Is there dessert?"

"Fresh peaches and vanilla ice cream."

"Then let's not bother with soup." He pulled out the cork, unwound it from the corkscrew. Then he scooped up the nearest glass, poured a little wine. He swirled the glass, sniffed the contents, tasted the wine. As he put down the glass he grinned at her, said, "But I am hungry," and hopped around the island toward her.

Alarm bells rang, and she knew she should move back. But before she could, he'd reached her and had grasped her hands. Her alarm intensified as he pulled her resisting body close to his. He looped his arms around her, and before she could wriggle free, had clasped his hands tightly together against the base of her spine.

"Zack, this isn't a good idea."

"I just want to talk." His eyes were warm, dark. His breath smelled of wine. "Look, I know it isn't easy for you, being here, seeing Arabella."

"It's only for a couple of weeks. I can handle it."

But could he handle being around his wife? Zack wondered.

He'd felt his whole body tighten as he'd pulled her curvy figure to him. Her perfume, the perfume that had aroused his curiosity in the elevator, was still as bold and sophisticated as it had been then, but whereas then it had turned him off, now it turned him on. It was a challenge. He needed to know if, below the successful-career-woman surface, there still lived the woman who had once loved him with such passion.

He had to move slowly, though. He mustn't frighten her. He had two whole weeks to find out what he needed to know.

So despite the fact that he wanted her so much it was driving him crazy, he brushed a kiss across the tip of her nose and released her.

He leaned against the island and gazed at her thoughtfully. She looked dazed, her eyes bewildered, her cheeks flushed, her lips full and moist...

As if they'd been waiting for, and ready for, his own.

He realized, with a shock, that despite her attempt to ward him off, she wanted him. Wanted him just as much, physically, as he wanted her. And it would be the easiest thing in the world to get her into his bed.

But he wanted more, far more than just sex.

He wanted her in his life as wife, lover, partner, soul mate. The way they had been before.

He wasn't sure, yet, how he was going to accomplish that. Or even if it was possible.

What he did know was that sex between them, at present, would be an empty thing. Hollow. Of no value.

Like this house, it was nothing without heart.

He knew Lauren's heart was frozen.

He had two weeks to thaw it. Two weeks before she left town for good. And he knew, deep down, that this was his last chance.

His very last chance to salvage their marriage.

CHAPTER FIVE

"AUNT Lauren?" Arabella licked her dessert spoon clean. "Is it too stormy to go tobogganing tonight?"

"It won't be much fun. Perhaps it might even be dangerous because the snow's falling so thickly we wouldn't be able to see where we were going. If it's not snowing tomorrow morning, we'll certainly—"

"Tomorrow morning," Dolly Smith said firmly, "Arabella and I shall go to church."

Zack cleared his throat. "The nearest church is ten blocks from here, Dolly."

"Then Lauren shall drive us!"

"That will depend on the state of the roads," Zack said. "And on whether or not Lauren *wants* to drive."

"Of course she'll want to drive! Won't you, girl?"

"I don't mind driving you, but as Zack says, it will depend on the roads."

"Don't they plow the streets around here? It's a fancy enough area, what I could see of it from the cab. What kind of taxes do you pay?" She glared at Zack.

Before Zack could respond, Arabella piped up.

"My mom always told me it was rude to ask people money questions."

Lauren heard a muffled sound from Zack, and when she glanced his way, she saw that he had pressed his napkin to his face. Out of the mouths of babes... She could almost read his thoughts as she saw the merry twinkle in his eyes.

"And did she not also tell you," Dolly snapped, her gaze sharp as an icicle point as it stabbed Arabella, "that it's the height of bad manners for a child to criticize her elders?"

"Let's put off making any decisions," Lauren said quickly, "until tomorrow. Zack, why don't you and Dolly finish your coffee in the sitting room, while Arabella helps me with the dishes."

As she spoke, she got to her feet. Scooping up cups and saucers, she scurried from the dining room. *Like the proverbial rat,* she reflected ruefully, *deserting the proverbial sinking ship!*

But if ever there had been an awkward meal, it had been that one. Dolly had refused a glass of wine, had asked tersely, "Where's the soup?", had found the chicken casserole too spicy. The ice cream had been too rich, the peaches too ripe, the coffee too strong.

She heaved a long sigh. She was glad to get away, for a few moments on her own. Peace and quiet.

In the sitting room she set Zack's coffee cup on the mantelpiece and Dolly's on the table next to an armchair before crossing to the window.

The storm was still raging, the powerful wind gusting violently against the panes, making them rattle.

She leaned a knee on the cushioned window seat as she watched the fat snowflakes slide down the glass. Her thoughts drifted to the past.

How often she and Zack had sat here with Becky, telling her the names of the constellations in the night sky. Her favourite cluster of stars had been the Pleiades.

The Seven Sisters.

And of all the stars in it, her very favorite had been

Maia. Not the brightest, but according to myth, Zack had told her, the first-born and most beautiful.

"Maia's got her sisters all around her. It must be nice to have sisters," Becky had said wistfully one night. "You'd never feel lonely."

And Zack, giving Lauren a sensual smile that had made her blush, had responded, "Your mom and I are working on that, sweetie. Let's hope you won't have too long to wait."

As she remembered, Lauren felt tears prick.

She blinked them away, and when she opened her eyes, she saw Zack's reflection in the window.

Her nerves tightened as he stopped behind her.

"Are you okay?" he asked. "Is Dolly getting to you?"

She made a derisive sound. "How can you *stand* her?"

He put a hand on her shoulder, and she felt the warmth of his fingertips on her neck, above the collar of her blouse. The touch sent spirals of sensation quivering through her.

She stiffened, and he dropped his hand.

"I can stand her," he said quietly. "What I *can't* stand is the possibility that she may get Arabella."

With a sigh, Lauren turned. He was so close she could smell the coffee on his breath.

"I do admire you," she said, "for not trying to pull the wool over Dolly's eyes."

"I was tempted. But as I said, it wouldn't be fair in the long run, not to Arabella nor to you."

"Nor to you, Zack." She hesitated, then said, "Do you mind if I ask you something?" He raised his brows and she braced herself to ask the question. "Are you... seeing anyone? Seriously, I mean?"

"No."

"Zack." She ran a trembling hand over her hair. "You mustn't hang on, hoping..."

"Hoping what?" His eyes had darkened.

"You know..."

"Hoping we'll get back together?"

She dug her teeth into her lower lip.

Anger sparked in his eyes. "I never wanted this separation in the first place! And you damned well know it!"

"Zack...you have to let go."

"Do I?" His jaw hardened. "And what about you? When are *you* going to let go?"

She swallowed but kept her gaze level. "I already have."

"I'm not talking about me," he said bitterly. "I'm talking about Rebecca."

She brushed by him then, moved to the middle of the room, stood with her back to him, her arms around herself tightly.

"I don't want to talk about Rebecca." Her voice was barely audible.

She heard the thump of his crutches on the carpet. He came up behind her, grabbed her arm, turned her around. She averted her head.

"You'll end up like Dolly Smith!" His fingertips dug into her flesh. "Loving nobody, nobody loving you. Dried up in your own grief!" He gripped her chin, made her look up. "Is this what Becky would have wanted?" he demanded harshly. "Do you think she'd—"

He stopped abruptly as Dolly's rasping voice preceded her into the sitting room.

"Come along, child, stop dawdling in the hall. Ah, there you are, Zack. I wondered where you'd got to." With regal hauteur, Dolly walked to her armchair and after arranging the folds of her long skirt, sat down.

"Arabella," she ordered, "please hand me my coffee."

Arabella trailed across the room, her expression despondent. "Yes, Great-Aunt Dolly."

"And then go up to my room and bring down my knitting." As Arabella trailed away, the elderly woman reached into her bag for her handkerchief and blew her nose. "I see you've no television in here. Thank heaven for that! An invention of Satan himself!" Thin nose quivering, expression self-righteous, she stuffed the handkerchief into her bag and lifted her coffee cup from its saucer.

Zack looked at her, then looked at Lauren.

His message was clear. Is this the way you want to end up?

And being the coward she was, she fled.

"What did Great-Aunt Dolly want to talk to you about when she sent me upstairs this afternoon?" Arabella dried the dessert plate and set it on the kitchen table.

Lauren looked into the small freckled face upturned so trustingly to hers. "Well—" she tried to think of the best way to explain "—she wanted to know if your uncle Zack and I were...back together."

"But you're not, are you."

Lauren shook her head. "No, we're not."

"But if you were, would she have gone home?"

"She might have."

"Why doesn't she think Uncle Zack could look after me properly? Doesn't she think he'd be a good dad?"

"I'm not sure what her reasons are. But if that's what she thinks, she's wrong. Your uncle Zack is just made to be a dad. He's always wanted to have a really big family, lots of kids, because he never had a real family when he was growing up."

Lauren was scrubbing the casserole dish in hot soapy water. Her hands stilled as memories flooded her mind. Memories of the day Zack proposed to her. Memories of what he'd said to her after she'd blissfully accepted his proposal.

"I want babies, sweetheart." He'd pulled her close against his heart. "Lots of babies. I want a big house, and I want to fill it with kids and sunshine and laughter."

"Oh, Zack," she'd said eagerly, "I do, too!"

"We're going to be so happy. We're going to be the happiest family on earth."

"Aunt Lauren?"

Startled, she looked around.

"I've finished drying all the plates and cutlery. What else can I do to help?"

"Nothing, thanks. I'll dry this casserole myself."

"Is it okay if I go into the den and watch TV?"

"Sure."

"I'll have to watch it a lot while I'm here." She hung her towel on the rack and heaved out a wistful sigh. "If I have to go back to Great-Aunt Dolly's, I won't get to watch it at all because she doesn't have a set. And at the Sheldon School for Girls, the only programs we get to see are documentaries!"

Lauren let Arabella stay up till nine, and shortly afterward, Great-Aunt Dolly tucked her knitting into her blue corduroy knitting bag.

"Early to bed, early to rise," she said with a virtuous sniff of her thin nose as she rose to her feet. "I should be obliged, girl, if you'd bring me a cup of hot water each morning at seven, after which I shall have my shower and shall be in the dining room for breakfast at seven-thirty sharp. Strong tea, two slices of hot toast and butter."

Zack had risen to his feet. "Will that be all, Dolly?" His tone was tinged with irony. The irony obviously escaped her.

"That will be all," she replied. "Good night, both."

After she'd gone, Zack muttered "Hallelujah!" and dropped into his seat.

Lauren put aside the magazine she'd been skimming. "How long do you think she plans to stay?" she asked.

"Your guess is as good as mine."

"What's her story, Zack? I mean, why do you think she is the way she is?"

He leaned back in his armchair, narrowed his eyes and looked at her with a veiled expression that made her feel uneasy. "You really want to know?"

"Yes."

"Okay." With both hands he raked back his hair, then clasped his fingers behind his head. His eyes never left hers, and with every second her uneasiness intensified. "Dolly Smith was born in England and grew up in London. She and her childhood sweetheart got engaged when they were both sixteen and they started saving to get married, but Jack was called up when he was eighteen—National Service—and not long after that the

Korean war broke out and his regiment was sent overseas. Jack was killed a couple of years later, just a week before he was due home for good. Dolly had made all the arrangements for their wedding.''

"Oh, how sad!" Lauren felt a pang of sympathy. To have loved and to have waited so long, so patiently...and then to have lost that love. "But that was—" she did a quick mental calculation "—forty-five years ago. So what happened next?"

"What do you mean, what happened next?"

She frowned. "Well, forty-five years. What did Dolly do, once she'd, you know, gotten over—"

"Nothing happened next." Zack's eyes seemed to drill right into her. "Oh, I'm not implying life stood still. She emigrated to Canada with her parents when she was twenty-five, then they moved to California, where they opened a high-class restaurant. Dolly took chef courses and eventually supervised the kitchens, and after her folks died, she took over the whole operation."

"I didn't know she'd been a chef!" Lauren grimaced, and in an attempt to lighten the atmosphere, added with a chuckle, "That explains why my dinner tonight didn't quite cut it!"

Her attempt at humor fell flat. Not even a twinkle lit Zack's eyes.

"She retired when she was sixty. Since her parents' death, she's been living on her own."

Lauren found herself wanting to wriggle uncomfortably under Zack's steady gaze. Where was he going with this? "So...she never met anyone else?"

"No, she never met anyone else." He shot forward from his relaxed position and set his hands on his thighs. "She never met anyone else because she didn't look for anyone else. That's what I meant when I said nothing happened next." His voice had become harsh. "Dolly Smith has wasted almost half a century living with a ghost! And that's what's going to happen to you, Lauren. Don't you see?"

He lurched to his feet, grabbed a crutch to steady himself. "You're going to end up just like her…miserable, bitter, lonely. It's four years, for God's sake, since Becky died! How much longer are you going to grieve?"

He'd never forget the look on her face. He'd never forgive himself for having caused it.

As he got ready for bed, his heart ached unbearably, the image of her pain-filled eyes so vivid he almost hunched over as it floated in front of him.

"You don't understand." Her voice had been laden with sorrow. "You've never understood. She was part of me, Zack. *From* my body, *of* my body—"

"I loved her, too, Lauren."

"Oh, I know, I know! But…it's not the same for a man, no matter how much he loves his child. You want me to get over it… I'll never get over it."

He'd hoped so hard, hoped that at last they were going to have a second chance.

When he saw her sorrowful face, heard her tearfully spoken words, his hope, at last, had died.

He pulled off his shirt, flung it onto the bedside chair. She was really suffering, and it broke his heart.

She was right—he should let her go. The pressure he was putting on her was only adding to her burden.

He would tell her, in the morning, that she could leave. She could go to Toronto and look for a condo.

He might have to pull a few strings to get her on

another flight at such short notice, but if necessary he would, and he'd pay whatever it cost to help her on that first step to starting her new life.

After that, he could do no more.

The Point Grey house had five bedrooms upstairs. Arabella was asleep in one, Dolly Smith in another. Becky's room lay empty. Zack normally used the master suite...which left the fifth bedroom for Lauren, a small room facing west.

She moved about it silently, getting ready for bed. And once she'd put on her silk pajamas, she slipped along the corridor to check on Arabella before turning in.

The door creaked as she opened it. The night-light, plugged into a wall outlet, gave the room an eerie glow.

Arabella's head was visible, and her thumb was stuck in her mouth. Her auburn hair cascaded over her pillow. Her breathing was deep. Her *Goosebumps* book lay on the carpet, where it must have tumbled after she'd fallen asleep.

Lauren picked it up and placed it on the bedside table. As she did, she knocked over a Barbie doll, which Arabella had set up on the table, and it fell with a clatter.

Lauren held her breath. Arabella stirred, drew her thumb out of her mouth and sighed. Then she murmured, "Mom," turned over and threw a wiry arm over the duvet.

Her eyes had never opened, and within seconds, she was sound asleep again.

Lauren's throat ached as she tucked the arm under the duvet and tugged the cover up cozily. What a brave little girl she was. How lost and lonely she must feel.

Yet how undemanding she was.

Take her request to go tobogganing after dinner, for instance. When Lauren had scotched the idea, the child hadn't fussed or nagged, but had serenely accepted that it wasn't to be.

Lauren ran a tender gaze over the freckled face, the long amber lashes feathering the silky skin, the rosebud mouth, slightly parted. Tomorrow, she promised, regardless of the weather, she'd take Arabella tobogganing.

Dolly Smith could rant and rave. She could stomp off to church on her own, if she so desperately felt the need to go.

Arabella wanted to toboggan—therefore Arabella *would* toboggan.

Lauren ran a gentle hand over the luxuriant spill of hair. "Good night," she said softly, "and sweet dreams."

Next morning, the sky was blue, the air was crisp, and more than four inches of snow covered everything in sight—including the street, which hadn't been plowed.

"You'll have to give church a miss, Dolly," Zack said over the breakfast table as the elderly woman sipped the last mouthful of tea from her china cup. "Unless you'd like to borrow a pair of snowshoes!"

"Young man—" her gaze was as frosty as the weather "—I'll thank you not to be impertinent!" She whisked her napkin off her lap, folded it and slotted it neatly into her silver napkin ring. "I'm well aware that the roads are impassable. I shall listen to a church service on the radio, and Arabella shall listen with me!"

"I'm sorry, Dolly—" Lauren walked into the dining room with a pot of coffee "—knowing I wouldn't be driving you to church, I've promised Arabella I'd take her tobogganing.''

''Ah, well,'' Zack said smoothly as he got to his feet and, using his crutches, hopped around the table, ''a promise is a promise.'' He pulled Lauren's chair out for her. ''Lauren.'' He touched her shoulder. ''I want to have a word with you. Before you and Arabella go out.''

She glanced at him. ''Is there a problem?'' He was wearing a navy V-necked sweater over a white T-shirt, and the navy accentuated the darker ring around his gray irises. What beautiful eyes he had....

She dragged her gaze away and sat down.

''No problem.'' He swung to his seat.

As he sat, Dolly said, in her abrasive voice, ''You can talk to the girl now! I'm going upstairs to make my bed. When I come down, I shall expect you to have a radio set up for me in the sitting room.''

After she'd left, Zack said, ''Where's Arabella?''

Lauren felt uncomfortably aware of his gaze as he looked over her classically styled taupe sweater, her immaculately made-up face and her elegantly French-braided hair. She knew he liked her hair loose, sensed he'd guessed that her present sophisticated style of dress was part of her armor. Everything about her said Touch Me Not.

''Arabella?'' she said. ''She ate breakfast in the kitchen a while back. I think she's watching cartoons in the den. So, what was it you wanted to talk about?''

''When the roads are plowed, you're free to leave.''

She'd lifted her coffee cup. She stopped with it half-way to her mouth. ''Free to leave?''

''I appreciate your offer to fill in here for the next couple of weeks but I've finally realized how difficult this is for you. I know I can't manage around here on my own, but since Dolly has dug her way in here, she can start earning her keep. It'll only be till the new year. By that time I'll have hired a nanny, and I plan on getting a live-in housekeeper, too. At any rate, you don't have to hang around any longer. You can go to Toronto, hunt for a condo. I'll get on the blower right after breakfast, fix you up with another flight. Tomorrow morning okay? Or would you prefer to leave later in the day?''

Lauren's mind was reeling. She'd listened to what he had to say, but she was having a problem assimilating it. He was releasing her? He was setting her free to leave, to walk out of his life? This time, he wasn't going to try to stop her?

It was what she wanted. Wasn't it?

It should have made her dizzy with relief.

Then why didn't it? Why did she feel as if she were falling into space from the top of the world, falling into a bottomless void?

"Lauren?'' He waved a hand in front of her face.

"Oh, sorry.'' She managed a smile. "I...well, it was such a surprise!''

He frowned. "You don't look too happy about it. I thought that's what you wanted. What you wanted all along.''

"It...is.''

"Then?''

"It is what I want.'' She tried to make her voice firm. "You know I didn't want to stay on here. The longer I stayed, the harder it would be for us all when the break came. It'll be best for me if I go.''

"Right! So?''

"I'm worried about you, Zack. You warned me last

night that I'd end up like Dolly. Not loving, not loved. Don't you see you're in danger of doing the same thing? If you keep hoping that one day you and I may—"

"It's okay, Lauren." He set his hands, palms down, on the table on either side of his coffee cup. "I've done a bit of thinking, and you don't have to worry about that any more. I have to accept that we've come, at last, to the final parting of the ways. You see, I'm going to do my damnedest to get Arabella, but I do realize that if the judge rules in my favor, I'll have finally scuppered any chance of getting you back."

"It's got nothing to do with Arabella!"

"Oh, but it does. Now." His eyes were grayer than she'd ever seen them, the dark ring around the irises even more pronounced. "Lauren, let's go back for a minute to that day we were in Braddock's office. You turned white as chalk when he called us in together. I couldn't think why, at the time, but then you admitted you thought I was going to start divorce proceedings. The only reason I can think of for that reaction was that you still want me—"

He ignored her little sound of protest and went on. "And you still love me but you're holding back because you're afraid. And you're afraid because you've found out the hard way that love comes with no guarantees. You're in the insurance business—I guess you know that even better than I do. Facts and figures. The client's window breaks, she gets it replaced. Her heart breaks— hey, she's out of luck. There's no money on earth can guarantee against heartbreak."

Lauren jerked her leg aside as his foot touched it. "I still don't see why you're bringing Arabella into it."

"You're afraid of loving me, but you're even more

afraid of loving Arabella. The thought of becoming emotionally involved with her really terrifies you, doesn't it? Because of Becky.''

She felt her cheeks pale. "Zack, please don't—"

"For God's sake," he pleaded hoarsely, "be honest with yourself...and with me...for once!"

Her love for him was tearing her apart. The look in his eyes was shredding her soul. "Yes." The word came out in a whisper. "Yes, I'm afraid. Because of losing Becky."

He leaned back, and it was as if all the life had drained out of him. "If I had ever come to you—" his voice was defeated "—and said, 'Let's get back together again and it'll be just the two of us, no kids, till the end of time,' would you have considered—"

"Zack." Lauren felt tears clog her throat as she fought to control her sobs. "You've always wanted a big family. I wanted you—still want you—to have the freedom to meet someone else and one day to marry again and have what you've always yearned for, a house filled with sunshine and happiness and children!"

He stared at her and she could see, could actually see, the color seeping from his face.

"Good God!" His expression was haunted, his eyes stark with horror. "That's it, isn't it! You rejected me in the beginning because you couldn't cope with...what had happened. But then it was for a different reason! Lauren, tell me it's not true? Tell me that's not the reason you—"

She stumbled to her feet. "Zack, you're only thirty! You can meet someone else, get married, still have that wonderful family you've always dreamed about.''"

He thumped his fists on the table; veins bulged at his

temples. He lunged to his feet, grabbed his crutches and swung himself around the table till he was nose to nose with her.

Lauren cringed.

"What kind of a man do you think I am!" he stormed. "It was you I wanted...you I've always wanted! Children? Of course I wanted children! But that was the icing on the cake! Why the hell couldn't you have told me this sooner?"

Emotion throbbed with such intensity between them she could almost see the flashes of electricity in the air. "Because I do love you," she cried. "That's why! I've told you once and I'll tell you again...I want only the best for you, Zack. And you can't have that with me!"

"You do still love me." Zack's look was one of pure anguish. "I should have known it. Should have believed what my heart was telling me. But you should have told me before. You've left it too damned late!" His voice had become ragged. "You want me now, you have to want the total package. Arabella and I—we come as a team."

Lauren felt as if her heart was splintering. What a hideous mess she'd made of everything. What an appalling, unforgivable mess. She'd been mixed up before, but she'd never felt so tangled with misery as she was at this moment. She loved Zack, and she wanted him so badly it hurt. But now there was Arabella. She couldn't—wouldn't—let herself love Arabella. The risks were too great.

With a sob, she brushed past Zack and made for the door. He didn't come after her.

But then, she hadn't expected that he would.

CHAPTER SIX

"AUNT Lauren!" Scarlet-cheeked after a couple of hours of tobogganing, Arabella came to an abrupt halt as she and Lauren were passing the local recreation center on their way home. "Look!"

Their breath puffed into the frigid air like clouds of white smoke as they stood together. Lauren's gaze followed Arabella's pointing finger, and she saw that a corner of the parking area had been set aside as a Christmas tree lot.

Christmas trees meant trimming, parcels...memories. Things she wanted no part of.

"I'm sorry, Arabella." She made to move on. "I didn't bring my purse."

"Wait!" Tugging off one snow-caked emerald mitt, the child delved her fingers into her jacket pocket. "The lawyer gave me this—" she held up a ten-dollar bill "—before I left L.A. He said it was in case of emergencies." Her eyes had a gleeful gleam. "This is an emergency, right?"

Lauren swallowed. She felt trapped. But how could she possibly refuse the child a Christmas tree?

"It'll have to be a small one."

"Small is good, Aunt Lauren." Arabella's face had lit up like a beacon. "Small is just fine!"

Lauren looked around doubtfully at the deep snow. "But how will we get it home?"

"Uncle Zack's toboggan is strong, and there's two of

us, Aunt Lauren! We'll ask the man to tie the tree onto the sled, and we'll pull it all the way to Lindenlea together!''

An enormous snowplow came roaring along their street as they trudged alongside the house next to Lindenlea.

"Quick!" Lauren cried. "Let's get off the sidewalk!" They hauled the toboggan several yards up the neighbor's driveway and watched the plow go past. It left waist-high drifts in its wake, drifts that encroached on the sidewalk, forming formidable barriers.

"If we'd stayed on the sidewalk, we would've gotten totally buried!" Arabella said in awe.

"Now we're going to have to climb over—"

"Lauren Alexander!"

At the sound of her name, Lauren turned and saw a familiar figure tramping toward her from the garage end of the drive. Dressed for the weather in a bulky parka, jeans and boots, Janice Fleetwood was waving madly with one hand and dragging a snow shovel with the other.

"Janice!" Laurel greeted her old neighbor warmly. "How are you?"

"I couldn't believe my eyes!" The middle-aged woman dropped her shovel and enveloped Lauren in a bone-crushing hug. "How have you been, for heaven's sake! I was talking to Zack last week, and he never as much as hinted that you were getting back together! Oh, this is so wonderful! Wait till I tell Mort—he'll be over the moon.''

"We're not, Janice." An icy gust chilled Lauren's neck, and she flicked up her jacket collar against it. "We're not back together. I'm just here for—"

"Aunt Lauren's just here for two weeks," Arabella said. "Uncle Zack's probably going to be my new guardian, and Aunt Lauren has promised to keep me company for the holidays. We're going to have a *really* fun time together. Aren't we, Aunt Lauren?" She looked expectantly at Lauren.

Lauren felt a stab of dismay as she saw the happy, confident shine in Arabella's green eyes. Zack hadn't told Arabella she was leaving! She had assumed he had. He should have told the child! For the moment, she forgot all about Janice Fleetwood. She had to clear things up with Arabella. "Arabella-"

"Yes, Aunt Lauren?" The child's brow tugged down in a frown. "What is it?"

Lauren opened her mouth to tell her she'd be leaving later that day now the street was cleared, but even as she tried to decide how best to soften the news, she saw a shadow darken the green eyes, saw Arabella's thin shoulders become rigid, as if she was bracing herself for bad news.

Lauren felt a deep sense of defeat.

How could she possibly disappoint this child who had already borne so much disappointment in her short life?

She suppressed a helpless sigh.

And instead of uttering the words she'd meant to utter, she scooped up one of Arabella's mittened hands, squeezed it reassuringly and smiled.

"I was just going to tell Mrs. Fleetwood that we're going home now to set up our Christmas tree."

"It's a *lovely* tree," Janice said.

"Arabella chose it. We both think it'll be just right for the den."

"It surely will!" Janice said.

As they made to leave, Janice gave Lauren another hug, a tight hug, as if she never wanted to let her go.

"That man misses you," she whispered with a catch in her voice. "He misses you so darn much. We all do, Lauren! This street hasn't been the same since you left. I pray every night that you'll come back where you belong. And I'm gonna keep on praying that same old prayer till you do!"

Zack helped them set up the tree, but they decided to put off decorating it till after lunch.

Lauren served roast pork with creamed carrots, mashed potatoes, Brussels sprouts, gravy and apple sauce. She also served strawberry cheesecake—which she'd made the night before—knowing it was Zack's favorite dessert.

"That was one terrific meal," he said as Lauren rose to gather the dishes. "Wasn't it, Dolly?"

"Plain fare!" the elderly woman returned sourly. "But better than the pap they serve on the airlines these days."

"Damned with faint praise," Zack murmured for Lauren's ears alone as she collected his dessert plate.

Lauren bit her lip to hide a smile. Dolly had eaten a hearty meal, and despite her grudging comment had appeared to enjoy every morsel.

Zack pushed back his chair. "My turn for the dishes."

"Let's all do them!" Arabella said. "Well, not you, Great-Aunt Dolly, because you're a guest. But let's the three of us do them! Many hands make light work!"

"You're just in a hurry to trim the tree," Lauren teased.

And Arabella chuckled. "Yup, I guess I am!"

It was almost three before they had cleaned everything up. As they made their way from the kitchen to the den, Lauren suggested they invite Dolly to join them.

"I'll ask her," Arabella said, and scampered off.

"The old bat won't come," Zack said, as he and Lauren went into the den.

Lauren felt her heart ache as she looked around the room, which had always been her favorite spot in the house. Bay-windowed and cozy, it was furnished with leather sofas and armchairs in soft green, with a green and powder blue Indian carpet on the parquet floor and an antique rosewood armoire housing the TV set. The drapes were green velvet, and she pulled them against the darkening afternoon.

She sighed and said, "No, she won't come. She's a bit of a damper, isn't she?"

"You can say that again."

"She's a bit of a damper, isn't she!"

Zack grinned. He opened the doors of the armoire and switched on the TV. "Let's see if we can find some Christmas music. Ah, here we go."

Lauren watched as the picture appeared on the screen. A choir of small boys with beaming faces and neatly brushed hair. They were singing "Away in a Manger."

Emotion clutched her throat.

She swallowed hard and said brightly, "Where are the decorations?"

"Still in the same place."

"Have you...used them since...?"

"No. I've always put the lights up outside, but I've never bothered with a tree. You?"

She shook her head. "No, I've never...bothered."

Arabella came running breathlessly into the den.

"Great-Aunt Dolly says she's far too busy with her knitting to waste time putting silly baubles on a tree!"

"Silly baubles, my—" Zack bit the word off and said, "D'you want to get the decorations, Arabella? They're in the closet under the stairs. Right at the front."

"Sure."

"Do you need some help?" Lauren asked.

Arabella was already halfway out of the den. "I can probably manage," she called over her shoulder.

As soon as she was out of hearing, Zack said, "So when are you going home? I've been in touch with a travel agent. There's a faint chance I can get you on a flight tomorrow afternoon, but it's more likely you'll have to take the red-eye special. Will you mind traveling overnight?"

"Zack, we have to talk about this. Why didn't you tell Arabella this morning that I wouldn't be staying on?"

"You're the one who's leaving! Haven't you told her?"

"No."

"You haven't told her yet?"

"No, because—"

"Well, you'd better damned well tell her right now, not let the poor kid keep thinking you're going to be around!"

Lauren sighed. "It's too late."

"What do you mean, it's too late?"

"I *am* going to be around." Lauren stooped to pick up a couple of fir needles that had fallen to the carpet. When she straightened, it was to find Zack staring at her with a bewildered expression.

"Oh, Zack, I just couldn't tell her. We bumped into

Janice when we were out, and Arabella started telling her about the fun time she and I were going to have for the next couple of weeks.'' She twisted her face in an apologetic grimace. ''I realized you hadn't told her, and I didn't have the heart to. She's gone through so much already.''

Zack muttered something inaudible, under his breath. ''You're right,'' he said. ''We can't twitch her around like some damned puppet on a string! It's the last thing she needs. And this first Christmas without her parents, it's going to be a specially difficult time for her.''

''So…you don't mind if I stay?''

''You're twitching me around like a puppet on a string too, Lauren! I was just getting used to the idea that you'd be gone! You know something? It would have been a hell of a lot easier for everybody if you'd just dropped Arabella and me here on Saturday and left. But—'' he raised a hand to stop her automatic protest ''—she knows you're going to leave for good after two weeks, so it's okay by me if you stay, because she'll have no expectations of anything more…and neither will I. How does that old saying go? Blessed is he who expecteth nothing for he shall not be disappointed?''

''Zack, sarcasm doesn't suit you. Please don't—''

''Don't what? Don't let you know how I feel? Maybe if you'd been more open about *your* feelings a long time ago, all this could have been avoided!''

''Let's not go into that again. I don't want to argue.''

''No, you prefer flight to fight. It takes guts to fight!''

''Yes,'' she said, her voice almost a whisper, ''it does. And some people have more than others.''

He hissed out a low oath. ''Lauren, I'm sorry—'' He halted abruptly at the sound of approaching footsteps.

Arabella staggered into the room bearing an enormous cardboard box. As she thumped it down on the carpet, she glanced at the two adults and her eyes became wary. Her cheeks took on a pink flush.

"There are two more boxes," she said in a subdued voice and scuttled off fast, as if she couldn't wait to be gone.

Lauren sighed. "She senses the tension between us."

"Yeah." Zack rubbed a hand over his nape. "She's one smart kid."

"Zack, we both want her to be happy. Can't we put aside our own differences and just concentrate on giving her a wonderful holiday? How about declaring a cease-fire?"

"To hell with a cease-fire," he said gruffly. "Let's go all the way and make peace."

Peace it was, and the next hour passed quickly and happily.

Great-Aunt Dolly came to the den just as Lauren was fixing the gold-winged angel to the treetop.

Arabella, brow furrowed in fierce concentration, was draping threads of silver tinsel on the outspread branches.

Zack was sitting on a leather ottoman, packing away the cartons that had contained the delicate red and green balls and white-sparkled figurines dangling on the tree.

The TV was still on. The choir of small boys was singing "Silent Night."

Zack saw Dolly first.

He made a beckoning gesture. "Come on in."

Lauren turned. Dolly was standing in the doorway, her nose aquiver, her gaze fixed icily on the television set.

Arabella moved around the tree to address Dolly.

"We sang 'Silent Night' at our Christmas concert, but we sure didn't sing it as nice as these boys!"

"Nicely!" Dolly snapped. "Not nice!"

"Don't you think they're singing nice...I mean, *nicely,* Great-Aunt Dolly?"

The choir was singing the last few notes of the Christmas hymn. They looked like cherubs and they sang like angels. And the purity, the sheer beauty of their young voices brought tears to Lauren's eyes.

Dolly clicked open her bag and drew out one of her huge white handkerchiefs. She blew her nose long and loud, as was her custom, and then stuffed the handkerchief away.

"I've heard worse!" she said grudgingly.

Lauren thought she saw a suspicion of a shine in Dolly's black eyes. Had the singing actually moved the cantankerous old woman? But before she could make up her mind, Dolly said, "I've made us a pot of strong tea. It's in the kitchen. Arabella, bring the tray to the sitting room!"

She sniffed and wheeled round, stiff as a marionette, then swept off to the sitting room to await her afternoon tea.

"Did you notice—"

"I thought she—"

Zack and Lauren stared at each other.

"Well, well," Zack drawled, "maybe the old bat isn't quite as granite-hearted as she'd like us to believe."

"No," Lauren said thoughtfully, "maybe she's not."

"But no way is she going to end up with Arabella!" he growled.

"No," Lauren agreed. "No way in the world."

*　　*　　*

That evening, as Lauren was tucking Arabella in for the night, she heard a light tap on the door.

"Can I come in?"

It was Zack.

"I thought," she said, "that the stairs were going to be too much of a hassle for you."

"I'm getting the hang of these things now." He leaned on the crutches. "Besides, you know how it is— we all get used to sleeping in our own beds! And I'm sure you remember how comfortable that bed is!"

She felt the color rush to her cheeks, but there wasn't a thing she could do about it.

"I've just told Arabella I'd take her shopping in the morning," she said primly. "We have presents to buy, and if you like, I'll order furniture for the nanny's room. May I assume I have carte blanche as to how much I spend?"

"Buy whatever you want." He slid his hand into his hip pocket and took out his wallet. "Here's my gold card. You and Arabella have fun." He glanced at Arabella. "Hey, kid, how do you like sleeping in here?"

Arabella slid up a little and supported herself on one elbow. "It's really neat, Uncle Zack. The bit I like best is where the bed is, "cause I'm so close to the window I can look up and see the stars."

"Yeah?" he said. "So...what's your favorite?"

"Oh, that's easy. It's Sirius, the dog star." She chuckled. "I chose that one "cause I couldn't have a dog."

"Your dad was allergic to dogs and cats." Zack nodded. "Yeah, I remember. Bummer, right?"

"Anyway, I chose the dog star." She cocked her head. "Did Becky have a favourite star, Uncle Zack?"

"Oh, yeah…Becky liked the Seven Sisters. Isn't that right, Lauren?"

Their eyes met, and she knew his thoughts had flown back with her own. To times when the three of them, sitting on the window seat, had looked into the night sky and dreamed dreams.

"Yes." She managed a smile. "They were her favorites."

Arabella yawned and sank back on her pillows, and Lauren grasped the chance to change the subject.

"Time you were asleep, young lady!" She kissed Arabella's brow. But before she could pull back, two wiry arms twined tightly around her neck and dragged her close.

"Good night Aunt Lauren." Arabella's curly hair brushed Lauren's temples. Her sweet, milky breath fanned her cheeks.

Lauren felt a sudden urge to sink down on the edge of the bed and draw the child into a warm and comforting embrace. She resisted. Not only for her own sake, but for Arabella's, she had to keep her distance. It would make parting so much easier for both of them. And soon the child would have a nanny on whom to lavish all her love.

"Good night, sweetie." The moment she started to draw away, Arabella released her, obviously having learned her lesson at the airport. Her Aunt Lauren wasn't into hugs.

Zack swung over and tousled Arabella's auburn hair. "Good night, pumpkin. If I'm off to the office tomorrow before you're up, have a great day. Shop till you drop." He grinned. "Christmas comes but once a year!"

* * *

As he and Lauren left the bedroom, Zack felt his head pound with frustration. He was no expert on children, but he knew damned well that Arabella had been hoping Lauren would hug her back. And hold her tight. The way a mother would.

Angry words wanted to explode from his throat, but he managed to suppress them. His thoughts, however, weren't so easily squashed, and as he and Lauren made their way downstairs, he let them run rampant.

She was going through the motions of looking after Arabella, and she couldn't be faulted, as far as that went. She had taken Arabella tobogganing. She had brought home the Christmas tree the child had wanted. She had cheerfully helped trim that tree. And later she had spent an hour in the kitchen showing Arabella how to make shortbread cookies. No one could ever accuse her of being cold and distant to the little girl the way Dolly was. But she *was* holding something back. Oh, yes, indeedy! And what she was holding back was the very essence of herself, the sweet and generous passion that had stolen his heart so long ago.

She waited for him at the foot of the stairs as, crutches under one arm, he used the banister for support.

The chandelier lights made her blond hair shine like white gold. That topknot she'd twisted up—he itched to undo it. And he *would* undo it....

The cool look in her wide-spaced blue eyes told him that the moment for such an action was not at hand.

But the itch remained.

"Can I drive you to the office in the morning?" she asked.

"Heck, no, I'll call a cab. But thanks for the offer."

"What about the nannies? Are you going to be interviewing them in your office or at home?"

"I plan to do the preliminary interviews at work and then I'll have the most likely candidate come around here so she can meet Arabella."

"Is there anything I can do, Zack?"

"There's not much point in your getting involved in that, but actually there is something."

Her cheeks had flushed as he turned down her offer, and he'd seen a quiver of her lower lip. Hell, he hadn't meant to hurt her, but there was no point in having her look the candidates over. He and Arabella were the ones who were going to have to live with the woman they chose!

"Christmas is only five days away," he said. "I'm going to get a puppy for Arabella."

"What a lovely idea!"

"Jerry Macinaw—you remember him? My manager?"

"Yes, I remember Jerry. Do he and Bettina still live out in Aldergrove?"

"Yeah. They still have the farm. Anyway, Jerry's collie had a litter recently, and he still has a few for sale. If the roads are okay tomorrow evening, would you drive me out so I can take a look and choose one of the pups?"

"Of course. Arabella, too?"

"No, I want it to be a surprise." He grinned wryly. "Dolly can make herself useful by baby-sitting."

"Then we'll go out later in the week and pick up the puppy?"

"I'll get Jerry to bring it in on Thursday."

"A puppy." Lauren bit her lip. "We meant to get one, didn't we? Later?"

"Yeah, Becky wanted one in the worst way. But we told her she would have to wait till she was old enough to walk it by herself."

"Arabella's at the right age."

"Yeah, Arabella's at the right age. And it'll be good for her, at this time, to have something to cuddle."

Dammit, that had come out unthinkingly. But he knew Lauren had taken it as a criticism.

Her face had paled. "I know what you're saying Zack, and you're being unfair. I won't get involved with Arabella, but it's for her sake as much as my own."

"I didn't mean to criticize—"

But she didn't wait to hear his apology. Swirling away from him, she made for the sitting room. She could have taken off for the kitchen—but then he could have followed her, forced her to listen. She had gone to the sitting room because that's where Dolly was.

And she knew that with Dolly around, he was not about to pursue the matter.

Next morning when Lauren awoke, she saw she had slept in. It was a minute after seven, and Dolly would be sitting up in bed, her expression sour, waiting for her hot water!

No time to have her shower and get dressed, as she normally did before starting her morning routine. She snatched her pink satin robe and tied it hastily around herself, dragged her tumbled hair from her face and hurried from the room. Zack had said he was leaving early. Thank goodness he'd already be gone.

The kitchen was deserted, but the pleasant smell of

coffee permeated the air and a mug was upturned on the draining rack beside the empty coffeepot.

Lauren filled a china cup with cold water, stuck it in the microwave, pressed the small numbered pads that would give it two minutes at high. She switched on the ghetto blaster Zack kept on the counter, and immediately the kitchen came alive to the sound of "Jingle Bell Rock."

She flicked open the mini-blinds and looked out.

The sky was blue, and water dripped from the eaves. The snow was melting. The roads would be fine for her shopping trip with Arabella and for her trip that evening with Zack as long as the temperature didn't drop and the highway become icy.

"Good morning."

Her heart gave a jolt. Zack. She hadn't heard his approach because of the radio.

She turned and saw him standing in the doorway, leaning forward on his crutches.

He was wearing his black leather jacket, a silver gray turtleneck and a pair of charcoal gray cords, the right leg ripped up from the hem to allow him to drag it over his cast. How many pairs of slacks and jeans would he wreck before he got it off, she wondered abstractedly?

She slid her hands into her pockets. "I thought you'd already left!"

But he wasn't listening. His eyes were all over her, caressing every inch of her like warm, probing fingers. Taking in her hair, all tousled, her face free of makeup, her robe, clinging to her breasts like a coat of pink paint.

And revealing the telltale jut as they peaked in tingling response to his warm and careful attention.

Oh, damn!

She drew her hands from her pockets and folded her arms around herself. And felt the engorged nipples press like mistletoe berries against her wrists.

"Isn't it time you were away?" She sounded as if she'd just run round the block ten times.

"I'm waiting for my cab." The timbre of his voice was rough. "Should be here any minute."

"Good."

His jaw tightened, his eyes narrowed. He took a deep breath, and she sensed he was about to swing his way over to her. She shrank against the granite-topped counter and felt the edge dig like a knife into her flesh.

"Zack..."

"Turn that damned thing off! I can't hear myself think!"

Afraid to take her eyes off him in case he lunged at her, she reached over, blindly searched for the black button and silenced the radio.

"You look," he growled, "the way I remember you."

"I should have showered before I came down." She babbled to cover her nervousness. "But I didn't want to take the time because Dolly likes her hot water at seven and I didn't waken till after seven and so I just grabbed my robe and didn't even brush my hair..." As if reminded of how untamed it looked, she dashed her hands through it, then remembered she wanted to hide her breasts and swiftly hugged herself again. "Or..."

The microwave beeped, and she jumped.

"Oh!" She latched gratefully onto the sound. "It's ready."

She crossed to the microwave, and as she walked, she felt as if her legs were turning to jelly. She set the cup of hot water on a saucer and made for the door. Zack still stood there. She knew she had to pass him.

But he didn't move aside.

"Excuse me." She looked into his eyes. "You'll have to move a bit to let me pass. I don't want to spill. It's scalding hot...."

He leaned over and kissed her on the lips. The cup rattled in the saucer. She wanted to jerk away but knew she couldn't. Scalding water would have spilled down both of them. He had her trapped, and he knew it.

The kiss went on and on and on. She could feel the steam rising from the cup, misting her chin. She could feel the steam rising from inside her, searing her blood.

Then she felt nothing but his lips moving on hers, warm and familiar and wonderful as they had always been. He was the best kisser in the world, sweet and passionate and demanding. He touched her nowhere else except her lips, but every nerve was screaming, every defense wilting. He smelled of after-shave and shampoo and desire.

She wanted to sink to the floor and drag him with her.

"Whew!" His awed murmur met her ears as he pulled back at last. "That was some hot kiss!"

"And that," Lauren said shakily as she heard the blast of a car horn, "is your cab!"

He grinned. "Saved by the bell!"

"Yes," she retorted as she sailed past him, "I was!"

"It wasn't you—" his amused voice followed her along the corridor "—I was referring to!"

She blushed as she stepped quickly up the stairs. Had he read her mind? Had he realized she'd been, at that moment, his for the taking?

It had been like old times, she thought with aching

nostalgia. The two of them in the kitchen together, she in her robe, he ready for work. On more than one occasion, a kiss like the one they'd just shared had led them to go back upstairs, kissing, kissing, all the way. If only it could be like that again, she thought wistfully.

"Hi, Aunt Lauren!"

She looked up, and there was Arabella standing on the landing, eyes sleepy, mouth open in a wide yawn.

Reality hit Lauren like a savage slap.

It could never be like that again. Zack had made it sharply clear that he and Arabella came as a package.

It was a package she could not afford.

CHAPTER SEVEN

AFTER breakfast was over and Lauren had finished tidying the kitchen, she went looking for Dolly.

She found her sitting rigidly in her armchair by the fire, her knitting needles flashing furiously. Arabella was at the window. She had set up a row of Barbies on the sill so they could see the pine siskins, house finches and red-breasted nuthatches visiting the sturdy wooden bird feeder that hung from the apple tree.

"Dolly?" Lauren hovered in the doorway.

"Yes?" Dolly said tersely without looking up from her knitting.

She was still in a snit, Lauren reflected with a sigh, because her cup of hot water had not arrived on the dot of seven.

"Arabella and I wondered if you'd like to come downtown with us. We're going Christmas shopping. We'll be leaving shortly. We want to get to the stores early, before they get too crowded."

Dolly jerked up her head and fixed Lauren with a hard, black gaze. "Christmas—" her thin nose quivered like a hyperactive rabbit's "—is not about shopping."

Arabella turned from the window. "Well, part of it is, Great-Aunt Dolly. I mean, the gifts themselves are fun, but it's what's behind the gifts that counts."

"Shopping is all about spending money!" Dolly snapped.

"Shopping *is* about spending money," Arabella

109

agreed, her expression thoughtful, "but giving gifts is all about love. When you spend time searching for something that's going to be perfect for the other person, that means you really care about them." She turned to Lauren. "Right?"

"Honey—" Lauren kept her tone light "—it's a yucky wet day out, and I'm sure Great-Aunt Dolly will be much happier staying here by the fire than traipsing around. How about you get your jacket and boots on, and we'll be on our way?"

"Sure."

Arabella smiled at Lauren as she left, obviously bearing no ill-will toward Lauren for not backing her up in her argument. She was as sunny as Dolly Smith was sour.

Guiltily, Lauren felt relieved that Dolly had turned down her invitation, for her unpleasant attitude would have spread a wet blanket over their outing.

'We may have lunch downtown," Lauren said. "Will you manage here on your own?"

"I've been managing on my own, girl, for more years than I care to count."

"Dolly?"

"Yes!"

"I should appreciate if you would stop calling me *girl*. I'm a mature woman—"

"Then for pity's sake, act like one!" Dolly thumped her knitting on her lap. "What's the matter with you, anyway, that you walked out on your man? You made vows, didn't you, when you married him? Vows that you broke and tossed away like straws in the wind."

"I had my reasons—"

"Reasons? Huh! You couldn't take what fate handed

out! No backbone! You lost your child, and that was a tragedy. But it wasn't only your tragedy, it was your husband's, too! And Zack Alexander had enough rejection as a boy without your adding to his pain. So I'll call you *girl* till the day comes that you stop running and face what fate dishes out to you!''

The attack was so fierce, so unexpected, for a moment Lauren felt numb. And then, as she realized the full import of what Dolly had said, she felt anger explode inside her.

''You have no right to talk to me like that!''

''Well, somebody has to! Zack's father walked out of his marriage when Zack was three, and the boy's mother made his life hell after that because he looked like his father and she couldn't stand the sight of him. But I guess you know all that. He'd have told you the whole story. He was never a one to keep secrets. All that boy ever wanted was to be part of a real family, and I guess you know that, too. He thought he had one when he married you, but he never figured you out for the lily-livered type. Can't say as I did, either, when I met you at the wedding. But then, you never can tell.'' She picked up her knitting. ''No,'' she said scornfully, ''you just never can tell.''

She concentrated on her work, her hands moving the needles so fast her fingers were a blur. As far as she was concerned, Lauren could see, the conversation was over.

Well, as far as Lauren was concerned, it was not!

''You're a fine one to talk,'' she said steadily, ''about the lack of backbone. The way I heard it, after your fiancé died—and that was a terrible tragedy, too—you shut yourself off from the rest of the world not for a few years, but forever! Where do you get off criticizing—''

"Aunt Lauren?" Arabella's voice, high with excited anticipation, came from the foyer. "Are you ready?"

For a long moment, Lauren gritted her teeth and watched Dolly, waiting for a response.

But Dolly said nothing. She glanced up briefly, her eyes flat as matt black paint. "Well, go on, girl!" she said curtly. "Don't keep the child waiting!"

Lauren opened her mouth to say something she knew she'd live to regret, but before she could utter the angry words, she felt Arabella poke her in the spine.

"Aunt Lauren?"

Lauren heaved a frustrated breath.

"Coming, honey."

She went into the foyer and slammed the door—firmly but not violently—behind her. Just hard enough so that Dolly Smith would know how royally ticked off she was!

"Just give me a minute to get my coat," she said to Arabella, and forced a smile, "then I'll be ready."

They shopped at the Pacific Centre Mall for three hours, stopped for lunch, and then shopped again. By the time they returned to the car, both laden down with packages, it was after two.

"You didn't buy anything for Uncle Zack," Arabella said as they tumbled their purchases into the Mercedes's trunk. "How come?"

Lauren closed the trunk. "I'm not quite sure what to get him. But don't worry, I'll think of something before Friday."

As they drove onto Burrard and got caught up in the stream of traffic surging south, Arabella chatted about the presents they'd bought, including the elegant crimson velvet cape Lauren had purchased for Dolly.

"She never wears anything but black," the child said doubtfully. "Do you think she'll like it?"

"I hope so. She'll look really nice in red, with her silver hair. Besides, it's a Christmas color. It'll perhaps make her feel more...well, cheerful!"

But despite her optimistic tone, Lauren didn't hold out much hope that Dolly would like the crimson cape. Darn it, she hadn't even meant to pick that one! She'd called the clerk over and pointed to the black one. At least, she'd thought she'd pointed at it. But her finger—of its own accord, she could have sworn—had swung like an arrow to the other stack, the one that glowed red as Christmas lights.

She'd still been blinking in bewilderment as the clerk started to wrap the thing. And then she thought, what the heck! If Dolly didn't like it, she could always change it!

They were crossing the Burrard Bridge when Arabella said, "What will Uncle Zack say when you tell him how much money we've spent?"

"He'll probably say, 'Is that all?'"

"Is he absolutely loaded?"

"Oh, yes, he's absolutely loaded."

"My mom and dad didn't have that much money. Our house wasn't insured for forest fires. But they left enough to pay for boarding school and then university. And if Uncle Zack hadn't wanted me, then I'd always have had a home with Great-Aunt Dolly." Arabella paused and then said, cautiously, "Do you like her, Aunt Lauren?"

Lauren glanced over her shoulder, then changed to the

inside lane as they started up South Granville Street. "In some ways I admire her," she said, avoiding a direct answer. "She says what she thinks, and most of us don't, at least, not all of the time."

"But sometimes, if you say what you think, you hurt the other person."

"Yes, you run that risk."

"Do you always—ooh!" Arabella broke off and leaning forward as far as her seat belt would allow, stared at a long, low building up ahead to the right. "There's Alexander Electronics! Could we stop by and say hi to Uncle Zack?"

"Oh, I don't think—"

"Please, Aunt Lauren? I know he'd want us to."

"Honey, it's time we were getting—"

"There he is!" Arabella screamed. "Uncle Zack! Uncle Zack!"

Oh, Lord, yes, there he was, swinging along the busy sidewalk on his crutches. The rain had stopped, but it was very breezy, and the wind was ruffling his black hair.

"Quick, Aunt Lauren," Arabella shrilled, "beep your horn!"

Lauren hesitated, and eagerly Arabella leaned over and pressed her fingertips down hard on the horn.

They were almost alongside Zack now. He, like a few others, turned his head automatically as the horn blared.

Arabella was jumping up and down in her seat. "Stop, Aunt Lauren! Stop, stop, stop!"

Lauren wanted to keep going. She kept her foot on the accelerator and stayed right behind the car in front.

"Aunt Lauren, there's a spot right ahead! With a meter! Please! Uncle Zack's waving us to pull in!"

Lauren grimaced. "I guess I'm outnumbered!" Flicking on her signal, she slowed and pulled into the vacant spot.

"Oh, goody! He's coming over!"

Lauren suppressed a sigh and rolled her window down as Zack rounded the hood to her side. He flattened himself against the vehicle as a bus lumbered by, then he swung himself to the door. Leaning on his crutches, he tucked his head down and looked in the open window.

"Hi, there," he drawled. "Finished shopping?"

"Yes!" Arabella piped up. "Can we come in and visit your office?"

His eyes locked with Lauren's. "What do you think?" he asked softly. "Do you have time?"

All the time in the world, she wanted to say as she looked into warm gray eyes that reduced her insides to mush.

"I guess," she said with an indifferent shrug, "we could pay you a quick visit."

He grinned at Arabella, and without looking around, Lauren knew the child was grinning right back at him.

Then he checked that the lane he was standing in was free of oncoming traffic before opening her door.

"Out you get," he said, "and I'll feed the meter."

As Zack ushered them into his spacious office with its charcoal carpet, white walls, modern paintings and art deco furniture, Lauren saw that it hadn't changed.

But when her gaze flicked to the brown-haired young woman in a short-skirted navy suit who was stooping over a low filing cabinet by the window, she reflected with an odd twinge in her heart that something *had* changed.

Zack had a new secretary.

At least she was new to Lauren.

The woman who had worked here before—the highly efficient salt-and-pepper-haired Ms. Agerton—had been stout and in her early sixties and was probably now retired.

This woman was much younger than Harriet Agerton, much more slender than Harriet Agerton, and that perky little bottom, so blatantly presented to them, most certainly did not belong to Harriet Agerton.

"Patsy?" Zack said as he swung past Lauren.

The young woman looked around. And Lauren saw, with an unpleasant sinking sensation in her stomach, that unlike Harriet Agerton, this secretary was extremely attractive.

When she saw Zack, her face lit up and she gave him a dimpled smile. Sliding the drawer in, she straightened, her curly brown hair dancing over her shoulders. Her suit jacket was unbuttoned, revealing apple-round breasts under a powder blue shell exactly the same shade as her wide eyes.

"Lauren—" Zack glanced at her briefly before turning again to his secretary "—I'd like you to meet Patsy Sweet. She's the one who keeps things going around here. I don't know how I ever managed without her! Patsy, this is Mrs. Alexander and—" he touched Arabella's head "—Arabella."

Patsy smiled. "Hi, Mrs. Alexander. So pleased to meet you."

"You, too," Lauren said, hoping she sounded friendly.

Patsy directed her attention to Arabella. "Hi, honey. Your uncle Zack tells me you've come for the holidays, all the way from L.A., and he's hoping you can stay for good. Are you having a fun time? Did you enjoy the snow?''

Lauren didn't hear what Arabella replied. She was too busy wondering just how much of his private life Zack shared with this woman. How much of his leisure time he spent with this woman. He'd told her he wasn't involved seriously with anybody. But he could be involved with her in a no-strings relationship. He had, of course, every right to be involved in any kind of a relationship he wanted—

''Patsy,'' he was saying, ''were there any messages while I was out?''

''Nothing I couldn't deal with,'' she assured him. ''Mrs. Alexander, would you like a cup of coffee? Tea?''

''Thanks.'' Lauren forced a smile. ''But Arabella and I just had an ice cream at the mall.''

Zack nodded. ''Okay. Patsy, would you phone Sandy and postpone our meeting? Tell him I'll call him when I'm available.''

''Will do.''

The secretary was wearing perfume. Just a hint. Lauren hadn't even noticed it till the woman passed on her way out. But after the door had closed, the scent lingered, sensually elusive and voluptuous. Jasmine and iris. Musk and amber. Seductive. Haunting…

Did she wear it for Zack?

Or for some other—

''Lauren, are you listening to me?''

She blinked. ''Zack. Sorry, I was— What were you saying?''

"I was saying I interviewed a couple of nannies this morning but neither one was suitable."

"What was wrong with them, Uncle Zack?" Arabella had seated herself on the swivel chair behind the big desk and was whirling casually around.

Zack leaned on his crutches and looked at her. "The first said she liked to eat little girls for breakfast and the other said she preferred to eat them for dinner!"

Arabella giggled. "You're just kidding, Uncle Zack."

"So you have how many more to see?" Lauren said.

"Three. One's coming in early tomorrow, and then I'll see the last two on Thursday."

"Let's hope one of them fits the bill." Lauren had lowered her voice so Arabella wouldn't hear, but the child seemed to have lost interest in the conversation and was fiddling with Zack's desk calendar. "You have to get somebody soon!"

"You think I don't know it?" His chin was set grimly. "The more I see of Dolly Smith, the more I'm determined she'll never get control of Arabella."

"There are other agencies." She tried to sound encouraging. "Surely it can't be so hard to find a nanny!"

"I'm not looking for just *any* nanny." His stare was almost belligerent. "I'm looking for the next best thing to a mother. And as far as I can gather, that kind of person's as scarce as hen's teeth!" He waved a dismissive hand. "I didn't invite you in here to listen to my problems." He swung around. "Hey, Arabella, would you like to go through the factory? See where all the real work gets done around here?"

"Sure, Uncle Zack!" Arabella slid off the chair. "I'd like to see the factory."

Patsy was at her desk in the exterior office.

She looked up with a smile as they passed by, and Lauren sensed that she watched them with her lovely powder blue eyes till they disappeared from sight.

She wanted to ask Zack if he ever took the woman out.

And she knew hell would freeze over before she let the question pass her lips!

"Where are you and Uncle Zack going?"

Dinner was over, and Arabella, sitting cross-legged on Lauren's bed, asked the question as she watched Lauren tuck a pink wool blouse into the waistband of her blue jeans.

To choose your Christmas puppy, Lauren could have said, but of course didn't.

"Just for a drive." She crossed to the dressing table and picked up her hairbrush. Dragging it through her hair, she swept the glossy swathe back and secured it with a blue crushed-velvet scrunchie. Then she carefully applied silver-gray eyeshadow and a fresh coat of sunset-pink lipstick.

"I liked Patsy today. And I thought she was really pretty." Arabella tugged forward a strand of her auburn hair and looked disgustedly at it. "Did you?"

"Yes." Lauren put on a pair of silver hoop earrings. "I thought she was lovely."

"I wish I didn't have red hair."

"Your hair's gorgeous, Arabella. Lots of women would kill to have hair that color!"

"Uncle Zack says he likes it, too." She sounded amazed.

"Uncle Zack has good taste."

"He thinks Patsy's pretty."

Lauren's stomach seemed to drop three inches. Hating herself for asking, she said, "How do you know?"

"I asked him, and he said, 'Yeah, she sure is pretty.'" Arabella jumped off the bed. "I'm going to wrap my presents when you're out. When will you be back?"

"Around ten. You'll go to bed at nine, okay?"

"Yup, okay."

They went into the corridor.

"It was fun talking with you." Arabella put her arms around Lauren's waist and stole a quick hug. "Night, Aunt Lauren, see you tomorrow."

And before Lauren could catch her breath, she'd sped off toward her room, leaving Lauren wondering why she suddenly felt so depressed. Was the horrid sinking feeling caused by guilt because she hadn't given Arabella a hug? Or was it caused by jealousy because she knew Zack thought Patsy was pretty?

As she walked downstairs, she probed her soul for the answer, and came to the conclusion that she felt both guilty *and* jealous.

No wonder she was depressed!

Downstairs she went looking for Zack.

She walked toward his study. The door was ajar, and as she approached, she heard the murmur of his voice. She knocked lightly and pushed the door wide.

He had his hip hitched on the edge of his desk, the phone to his right ear. At the sound of her tap, his head jerked up. He frowned. His eyes took on a wary look. As if he wondered how much, if anything, she had overheard.

He put his hand over the mouthpiece.

"Would you mind? I won't be a minute."

For about four seconds, Lauren froze. What could be so private that he was dismissing her?

Then she felt her cheeks flame.

Swiveling, she left, her runners padding quickly along the corridor. Angrily, she paced the foyer, waiting.

What was it Dolly had said that morning when talking about Zack? *He was never a one to keep secrets.* Well, was Dolly ever wrong about him! Zack had made it quite obvious he didn't want anyone to know who he was talking to on the phone or what he was talking about!

And she would make it quite clear, if he brought the matter up on the way to Aldergrove, that whoever or whatever he was trying to hide, the matter was of absolutely no interest to her!

He didn't mention the phone call once.

In fact, he didn't seem inclined to talk at all. And since neither did she, the one-hour drive passed mainly in silence.

Only when they were at the farm and Jerry had taken them to the barn did they come out of their self-imposed silence. And how could it have been otherwise? The puppies were adorable, four little black and white bundles of fur, full of life and scrambling all over the straw.

Lauren had to chuckle when, instead of Zack choosing a pup, one of the pups chose Zack within twenty seconds of their arrival.

He was the second smallest, bright-eyed and full of fun. As soon as he noticed Zack, he tumbled over himself in his hurry to sniff Zack's outstretched hand. And once he'd done that, once they'd made friends, the matter was settled.

"Well, that didn't take long!" Laughing, Jerry

Macinaw leaned against the wooden stall as Zack scooped up the pup and stroked its back. "So...I'll bring him in to the office on Thursday." His brown eyes twinkled. "You'll get no sleep Thursday night. He'll cry like a baby. You can try all the tricks, of course, to keep him happy—hot water bottle, ticking clock..."

"They're all so cute, Jerry!" Kneeling on the straw, Lauren played with the remaining three pups. "I wish we could take them all!"

"You can't take one where you're going!" Jerry said. "Zack tells me you're off to Toronto in the new year. And you'll be looking for a condo. You've got a promotion?"

While Lauren briefly filled Jerry in, she wondered, just as she had with Patsy, how much Zack told his co-workers about his personal life. She never discussed her private life with anyone at Perrini Insurance.

"Sounds like a good posting, Lauren. I wish you well. Now—" he addressed Zack "—have you time to come into the house for that cup of coffee Bettina promised you?"

"Sure, but it'll have to be quick. The roads are busy, we've left Dolly baby-sitting and we don't want to be late."

Zack had always loved visiting the Macinaws.

And, he recalled as they trooped into the warm and cozy kitchen, so had Lauren. They had visited back and forth on a regular basis until Becky's death.

He hadn't been here since Lauren left him.

Bettina, in blouse and slacks with a striped vinyl apron around her waist, was taking a pan of cookies out of the oven. The air smelled of vanilla and almonds and coffee, from the pot on the counter by the stove.

The Macinaw children, boys aged four, six and eight, were in the sunken family room divided from the kitchen by two steps. They were watching a noisy TV sitcom. Saul, the eight-year-old, rolled round and called to Zack.

"Hey, Mr. Alexander, which pup did you pick?"

"Second smallest," Zack said.

"All right! You didn't choose the runt—Dad says we can keep him if nobody wants him!" Snatching a handful of popcorn from a big blue bowl in front of him on the carpet, he returned his attention to the TV.

Zack propped his crutches against the counter and pulled out a chair for Lauren at the round oak table. Then he sat beside her and automatically rested his arm on the back of her chair.

A mistake.

Over the homey kitchen scents, he smelled that sophisticated perfume she'd taken to wearing. It disturbed him...and challenged him.

Bettina said, "Jerry, hon, would you set out the mugs?"

Zack leaned sideways and whispered in Lauren's ear, "What the hell perfume is that you're wearing?"

"Don't you like it?" Her cheeks looked hot, but her gaze was cool. "Is it too...sophisticated? Maybe you prefer something with more oomph. Like the stuff your secretary wears?"

"Patsy?" He raised his brows, his eyes frankly curious. "How the heck did *she* get into this?"

"You take yours strong and black, don't you, Lauren?" Bettina slid a mug of coffee across the table to Lauren.

"Thanks." Lauren managed a smile. "You have a good memory."

"Zack—" Jerry looked at his boss "—would you come to my office for a minute? Something came up today after you left that I'd like to pass by you."

"Oh, sure."

"Here," Jerry said, "I'll carry our coffees."

"Thanks." Throwing Lauren a puzzled glance, Zack got up.

As Jerry walked past Bettina, he gave her a peck on the cheek. "Be right back, hon."

Bettina followed her husband with her eyes as the two men left, and after the door was closed behind them, she leaned against the counter, coffee mug wrapped in her work-roughened hands.

"What a great guy that Jerry is," she murmured, almost to herself. "And to think I almost lost him."

Lost him? What could she mean? Lauren frowned. "He didn't...start playing around, did he?" After all, she hadn't talked with Bettina for almost four years, and a lot could happen in that time.

"Jerry?" Bettina's chuckle was genuine. "He's the last man on earth to fool around. He's like Zack in that regard. No, I was talking about when we were first married. Years before you and I met. I don't think I ever told you this. Jerry and I... Well, for a long time it was too painful to talk about, and now we just concentrate on what we have. Each other and the boys."

"But...how did you almost lose him?"

Bettina reached behind her and set her mug on the counter. "Jerry and I had to get married. Oh, we'd meant to eventually—we were madly in love—but not quite then. I'd only just turned nineteen."

"But you're— You must be thirty-two now, aren't you?"

"I'm thirty-three, and Saul is only eight. It doesn't add up, does it?"

Confused, Lauren shook her head.

"Saul wasn't my first pregnancy, Lauren. He didn't come along till Jerry and I had been married six years. I miscarried the first."

"Oh, Bettina, I *am* sorry!"

"The loss of that baby almost wrecked our marriage. I just couldn't handle it. I rejected Jerry. I thought he didn't understand. How could he understand? The baby wasn't part of him, the way it was part of me."

Lauren had felt a welling up of compassion when Bettina said she'd lost her baby. But even as that compassion filled her heart and spilled over, a cold shiver iced her skin.

Bettina had never talked to her about this before. In all the years they'd known each other. Why was she telling her now? It was, Lauren reflected bitterly, no coincidence. No coincidence that she was here with Zack, ostensibly choosing a puppy. He had asked her to drive. He could have asked Jerry to drive. Jerry would have been delighted.

No. It was a setup.

Zack had planned for Bettina to share her story. The excuse Jerry had made to get Zack out of the kitchen was part of the setup. Anger and resentment flared inside her with an intensity that rocked her, and it was only with an enormous effort that she managed to rein in her fury.

"I kept pushing, pushing Jerry away," Bettina said, "and then, one day, by some miracle, I surfaced from my grief long enough to realize he was in as much pain as I was, and needing comfort as much as I was. I reached out to him...and that was all it took. For both of us. From then on, we've never been closer.'' Tears filled her eyes. ''When I look at the boys, at Saul and Jerry Junior and Todd... I just love them all so damned much, and to think that I—''

She stopped, tears rolling down her cheeks. She swiped at them ineffectively with her sleeve, and then with a watery smile and a choking sob, said, ''Excuse me for a sec, Lauren. I need a tissue—actually, I think I need a whole box of the little critters!''

She went out of the room, and a couple of seconds later, Lauren heard a door close. The bathroom door just a few steps down the hall.

Lauren lurched from her seat, her heart almost bursting with anger. Zack! How dare he do this to her! She would never forgive him. Her situation was far different from Bettina's. Miscarrying a baby was not to be compared with losing a child, a beautiful and adored and cherished four-year-old child! What did Zack hope to prove by—

She started as she heard Jerry's voice coming from the corridor. She quickly put on her jacket, scooped up her bag. When Zack and Jerry came into the kitchen, she was ready to leave.

Jerry looked around. ''Where's Bettina?''

''In the bathroom. Zack—'' Lauren's throat felt as rigid as if made of steel ''—we ought to be going. Dolly will be expecting us back.''

''You're the boss!'' Zack gave her a casual grin.

''Say goodbye to Bettina, Jerry.'' Lauren opened the outside door.

"Will do."

And two minutes later Lauren was driving the Mercedes along the narrow country lane that led to the highway.

She fixed her gaze on the road. She would say nothing to Zack till they got home. A right royal row lay ahead, and she didn't want to be driving when it happened.

CHAPTER EIGHT

Zack had sensed something was wrong the second he'd set foot in the kitchen.

As Lauren drove the Mercedes along the farm road to the highway, he saw that her fingers were clutched around the wheel so tightly her knuckles glowed like ivory in the dim light from the panel.

He braced himself for whatever shots she was going to fire at him, but when the tension-filled silence continued, he clicked on the radio and fiddled with the setting till he found a station playing Christmas carols.

As the speakers from the back filled the car with the cheery strains of ""Feliz Navidad,"" he adjusted his seat to a reclining position and closed his eyes. She would get to whatever was bothering her, he decided, in her own good time. Meanwhile, he had to wonder if what had sparked off her foul mood had been his remark about her perfume. Her hackles had risen, and she'd made that sneering comment about Patsy's perfume. For Pete's sake, what had Patsy or her perfume got to do with anything?

Women. He'd never understand them.

He'd hoped that by arranging this outing to the farm, they'd have a chance to communicate. He could have gotten Jerry to drive him out, but he'd wanted to spend time alone with Lauren. He'd also hoped that seeing the Macinaws and their three boys, the epitome of everything a family should be, would have softened her toward him.

But something had gone wrong.

Absently he whistled through his teeth in accompaniment to the voice on the radio. And waited for what was to come.

When they got home, it was after ten.

The first thing Zack noticed, when he switched on the hall light, was a sheet of paper on the hall table.

He swung over and picked it up.

"A note from Dolly," he said. The first words that had passed between them since they left the farm.

He read it aloud.

"'Arabella is in bed and asleep. I, too, have gone to bed and would appreciate it if you would make no noise.' Old bat," he muttered as he crumpled the note in his big hand and tossed it aside.

He turned and saw that Lauren had already hung up her jacket. She was looking at him with eyes that shone like glass.

"I have something to say to you." Her face was white save for the two patches of scarlet on her cheekbones.

"Yeah," he said. "I gathered that." He took off his jacket and hung it beside hers. Then turned to her again. "So, whatever it is, spit it out!"

"You are despicable." She didn't raise her voice. Her tone was deceptively controlled. If he hadn't seen the pulses throbbing at her temples, she might have fooled him.

"I am?" He rubbed a hand uneasily over his nape. *Despicable.* Hell, this was worse than he'd thought it would be. "Would you care to tell me why?"

"Taking me out to the farm tonight. The whole thing was a setup. Did you think I wouldn't guess what you were up to?" Her voice was still even, but traced with scorn.

"A setup?" He blinked at her. "For Pete's sake, what kind of a setup?"

"Don't act dumb, Zack. You know full well what I'm talking about. You got me out there under false pretences. Will you deny that you could have driven out there some time through the week with Jerry?

"No, of course I'm not denying it!"

"Then why didn't you?"

He glared at her. "Because I wanted to spend time with you, dammit!"

"Ah, but there was more to it than that!"

"Lauren." His voice grated with barely controlled impatience. "I really don't know what the hell you're talking about."

"No?" Her eyes flashed with fury. "You didn't put Bettina up to telling me about her miscarriage just so—"

"Hey, hey! Hold on a minute! You've lost me. Miscarriage? What miscarriage?"

She thinned her lips and made for the stairs. "Don't make matters worse by pretending innocence, Zack. I just wanted you to know I'm on to you. And I want you to know that what you did—using Bettina in that way—was beneath contempt. If you'd seen her, seen how upset she was…"

She started up the stairs. "I'm leaving, Zack." Her shoulders were stiff. "I don't want to stay here with you any longer. I'll explain—try to explain—to Arabella in the morning."

She had reached the landing. But he was right behind

her, propelled by boiling emotions that had lent him an agility with his crutches that astonished him. He reached out to stop her, but his hand missed by inches.

She marched determinedly along the corridor. He swung himself after her and caught up to her when she was almost at the closed door of her bedroom.

With one hand, he grabbed her by the shoulder.

"Not so fast!" He held her firmly and leaned against the wall. Damned crutches were getting in the way! He raised his elbows and nudged them free, and they fell outward, to land with two thumpety-thumps on the carpet.

Lauren was struggling to get away. He pulled her close. Closer than she'd been to him in over four years.

"Okay," he muttered. "Let's get this straightened out."

Her eyes glittered, and her voice was hard with accusation. "You *knew* Bettina and Jerry had to get married and that they lost the baby before it was born! You *knew* their marriage was rocky for a while after that because at first Bettina pushed Jerry away and—"

"I did nothing of the damned kind!" he returned. "But just supposing what you're saying is true—which it isn't—I still don't know why that would have made me despicable!"

"You thought that because Bettina had put the past behind her I should be able to do the same."

"You are the most infuriating woman I have ever met!"

"And you are the most insufferable man I have ever met!"

"The only thing I'm guilty of is wanting to spend time with you!" He wanted to shake her. "Got it? There was no setup. I wasn't aware of any of that stuff you told me about Bettina and Jerry. I just wanted—'' he did shake her, not too roughly but enough to slacken that idiotic velvety thing holding back her hair ''—I just wanted to be with you!''

Her eyes were wide, her lips quivering. Her hair was loose. With an explosive sound in his throat, he tugged the velvet thing off. Thrusting his hands through the glorious blond tresses, he spread them over her shoulders in a dazzling sheet of sunshine.

''Oh, sweetheart.'' The words came out on a groan. ''You are so beautiful....''

She'd been wriggling to get free, and as he spoke, her pelvis twisted against him. He felt a sharp tightening in his groin. She shuddered. He whispered her name and saw her eyes fill with tears.

He felt tears thicken in his throat.

Dear God, what were they doing to each other?

How had it ever come to this?

''Honey.'' He framed her face in his hands. ''Please don't cry.''

''Oh, Zack.'' A tear ran down her cheek, trickling warm on his index finger. ''I'm sorry I said those awful things. I really thought—''

He kissed her. And she melted against him like sweet honey. She flung her arms around his neck, and her breasts pressed to his chest. Her mouth was warm and mobile and seeking.

He kissed her till she came up, half-laughing, half-gasping for air. He caressed her hair, slid his hands down her spine, cupped her bottom and drew her even harder against him. They'd been married. They'd made love more times than he could ever count. And their bodies had always been made for each other. A perfect fit.

Her scent was hot in his nostrils, firing his blood. What was it about that sophisticated touch-me-not perfume that made desire sizzle through him? She parted her lips. He seduced her with his tongue. He heard her low moan. He reached sideways for the doorknob and turned it. Together, molded together, his arm around her for support, they moved awkwardly into the room.

He shut the door. It clicked with a light sound.

"You want this, Lauren?" he whispered huskily into her hair, hair that billowed like silk against his cheek.

"Oh, yes…"

Clinging to each other breathlessly, they made their way to the bed, he hopping, she stumbling, supporting him, kissing all the time, frantically kissing, he opening the buttons of her blouse, she sliding her hands under his shirt, tugging it from his pants. He felt her skin like warm satin on his fingertips, the sensuous texture intensifying the acceleration of his heartbeats and the urgency of his hands as he ran them over her ribs, up her back, sliding off the blouse—

She froze.

"Zack."

"Yeah?"

"Ssh. Listen."

He listened. And was about to say he couldn't hear anything when he heard it—the sound of someone breathing.

"Stay there," she whispered, and leaving him standing wobbling on one leg, she took off.

He heard the click of the door opening, and a sliver of light slanted across the carpet…and the bed.

Under the cover, a small shape was curled. Over the pillow, auburn hair glowed. On the nightstand, a Barbie stood watch. Atop a *Goosebumps* paperback.

"Oh, Arabella." Lauren's voice shook.

Zack heaved a frustrated sigh. "Yeah," he said, leaning a hand on the nightstand for support. "Oh, Arabella!"

"She must have felt lonely," Lauren whispered from the door. "Here alone with Dolly."

"I guess." He cleared his throat gently. "Are you... going to take her back to her own room?"

She could hear the question in his words, what he was really asking.

"No. There's no point in disturbing her."

"You sure?"

She nodded. "Hang on, I'll get your crutches."

She slipped out and in a second glided into the room and silently gave him his crutches.

In the slant of light from the door, their eyes met. The sexual tension between was so thick she felt herself choking in it. More than anything in the world she wanted to slide her arms around him, lean her cheek against his heart. And stay that way forever.

"Are you sure?" he said with a sigh.

She nodded. It was probably the hardest thing she'd ever done.

"You know where my bedroom is." He touched her hair, his gaze cloudy. "If you should happen to change your mind..."

"I won't, Zack." Her voice shook. "What almost happened just now...it would have been a mistake."

"Yeah," he said, and headed for the door. "I guess

you're right. But," he added softly over his shoulder as he went out, "you wanted it, just as much as I did."

Next morning, Lauren woke at twenty to seven.

She yawned, stretched out her legs...and became aware of another body in the bed.

Zack? Dear God, no! Surely she hadn't—

Heart in her throat, she jerked her head and peered desperately into the shadowy dark.

And in the filtered light from the window she saw the glow of auburn curls.

Arabella.

Relief flooded through her, making her sag weakly.

But on the heels of that relief, rushed memories. Memories of Zack's kisses. They had been so sweet, so passionate. So irresistible...

Arabella stirred, and Lauren held her breath.

The child twisted toward her, mumbled something in her sleep and flung out an arm. When it made contact with Lauren's shoulder, she snuggled closer and with a contented sigh, hooked a thin wrist around Lauren's neck.

It had happened so quickly, so unexpectedly, that Lauren didn't have time to avoid the sleepy embrace. She was trapped. Trapped with the milky scent of Arabella's breath in her face, the silky-soft brush of the child's hair against her bare neck.

Was there anything in the world more tender than a sleeping child?

Lauren felt something melt inside her. The way the first spring sunshine melts the surface of a lake's deep winter ice.

Tears blurred her eyes. She choked back a sob, and

unable to help herself, she slipped an arm around Arabella and pulled her close. Her body was tiny, fragile, cozy in her white cotton nightie.

"Aunt Lauren?" she murmured in her sleep.

"It's all right, honey," Lauren whispered and dropped a kiss on the pale brow. "It's not time to get up yet."

"I snuck in last night. I missed you...."

"It's okay, don't worry."

Arabella relaxed her grip around Lauren's neck. Her breathing steadied as she drifted back to sleep. Carefully, Lauren eased herself free and got up.

After she'd dressed, she stood for a long moment looking at the sleeping child, curled into a ball, her face half-buried in her plump white pillow.

Panic shivered through her.

She felt like an aerialist walking a tightrope, headed for safety. Determined to get to the other end without falling.

But despite her intention to remain uninvolved, she was finding it harder and harder to resist the child.

And loving Arabella was a risk she couldn't take.

Zack had left for work before she went downstairs, and she didn't see him again till that evening.

When he came home, she was in the kitchen preparing dinner. She heard him hopping along the corridor, and the warning sound gave her time to collect herself.

"Well, hi there!" he drawled as he came in. His eyes had a knowing twinkle that brought a blush to her cheeks.

"Hi," she said. He'd taken off his jacket and was wearing a navy turtleneck sweater and jeans. His cheeks had a healthy glow. His hair looked damp. "Is it still raining?"

"Yeah. And getting blowy. Gales forecast, I believe." He glanced around. "Anything I can do to help?"

"No, everything's under control."

"Everything...and everybody?" He raised a mocking eyebrow.

Her blush deepened. "Zack—"

He swung over to her. She stood her ground.

"Why the hell do you insist on scraping your hair up like that?" He raised a hand, and she knew he was going to take off her scrunchie.

She stepped back quickly, rounded the island and faced him across it. "Please don't."

He put his palms up in surrender. "Point taken." He poured himself a glass of water, drank it down and turned to her. "So...how was your day?"

"Arabella and I did some Christmas baking in the morning, and then after lunch I popped out to do some shopping. Just some last presents to buy." She wasn't about to tell him she'd been shopping mainly for him. "I bought a lovely book on astronomy for Arabella, since she seems so interested in stars."

She thought his eyes darkened a little. Was he thinking of Becky, who had also been so enthralled by the heavens?

But all he said was, "Good. And for the old bat? A belfry of her own?"

Lauren suppressed a chuckle. "A crimson velvet cape."

"I hope—" his gaze had become serious "—you haven't bought anything for me. You know that the only thing I want for Christmas is something money can't buy.''

''Zack, please—''

''How was Arabella this morning?'' He changed the subject bluntly. ''Did she explain why she was in your bed?''

''She was lonely.''

''Poor kid.''

Tension thrummed in the air. There had been only the faintest hint of reproach in Zack's tone, but it was enough to charge up her resentment.

''If you want to do something to help,'' she said coolly, ''you can tell Arabella to wash her hands. I'll be serving dinner in a minute.''

''I'm going to be out later this evening.''

Where are you going? ''Do you need a drive?''

''No, Patsy's going to be picking me up at eight.''

The green-eyed monster sprang to roaring life.

''Fine,'' Lauren said smoothly.

''You've been invited—''

''Thanks but wild parties aren't my scene.''

Her cold rejection of his invitation was almost drowned out as Arabella ran into the kitchen, her slippers flip-flopping on the floor.

''Uncle Zack! I *thought* I heard your cab pull up!''

''You heard right, pumpkin.'' Leaning on his crutches, he bent so she could put her arms around his neck, and they exchanged hugs. ''Dinner's ready. You go and get your hands washed and I'll tell your great-aunt Dolly to take her seat in the dining room.''

Their voices faded as they left the kitchen.

And Lauren was left wilting against the counter as her mind set out some facts that sank her into gloom.

(a) Zack was going out with Patsy.

(b) Zack thought Patsy was pretty.

(c) Patsy was good with children.

(d) Arabella liked Patsy.

(e) And Arabella needed a mother.

Lauren had never been particularly good at algebra, but no matter how many ways she added up these five factors, the answer she invariably came up with was (f).

And (f), as she knew only too well, stood for family.

When the doorbell rang at eight, Arabella was in the den watching TV, Dolly was in the sitting room with her knitting, and Lauren was in the sitting room arranging Christmas cards on the mantelpiece.

She ignored the bell.

The door was ajar, and she strained for the sound of Zack coming down the stairs. She heard nothing.

The bell rang again.

Dolly thumped down her knitting. "You deaf, girl? Get the door!"

Compressing her lips to keep back an angry retort, Lauren set down the cards in her hand and walked from the room. She hesitated in the foyer, but since there was still no sign of Zack, she went to answer the door.

She opened the front door expecting to see Patsy on the stoop. Instead she saw an athletically built hunk with a blond crewcut, rugged features and hazel eyes—eyes that smiled as he said, "Hi, there, Mrs. Alexander. I've come to collect Zack."

She looked past him and saw a shiny forest green Lotus in the drive. "I thought Patsy..." A faint frown tugged her brows together.

"The twins were running rings around the baby-sitter, so she's going to come along later in her own car once the holy terrors are asleep."

"Holy terrors?"

"Chuck and Dani. They've just hit the terrible twos—shoot, I haven't even introduced myself. I'm Ben, Patsy's better half. Her parents are throwing a party for us. It's our fifth wedding anniversary...."

He looked beyond Lauren, and she realized Zack had come downstairs.

"Hi, Ben," Zack said as he came up behind her.

"Hi, old buddy. Ready to go?"

"Sure." Zack came alongside Lauren and put an arm casually around her shoulders. "You two have met?"

Lauren stiffened. Had Zack realized she suspected he was sexually involved with Patsy? Had he guessed she was jealous? Did he know how embarrassed she felt now?

"Yeah," Ben said. "We've met. Hey, Lauren, you're invited, too. Patsy's folks would be pleased to have you."

"Are you sure you won't come?" Zack looked at her.

He was wearing a deep blue suede jacket that hung open, and under it was an icy blue crewneck cashmere sweater over a fine flannel shirt with a small check. He was probably wearing gray flannels or jeans with the right leg slit up one side, but she didn't look down.

"Thanks," she said stiltedly. "I've got a ton of stuff to do tonight, parcels to wrap and such."

"Okay, then."

She drew back as Zack swung his crutches forward. The two men headed for the Lotus.

"Don't wait up," Zack called over his shoulder. "I may be late."

She had just closed the door and gone into the foyer when Arabella appeared, her expression eager.

"Aunt Lauren, look what I found!" She held out a video. "It says—" she squinted at the label, printed in handwriting that Lauren recognized as her own "—Becky's Birthday Parties. Can you play it for me?"

Lauren stood at her bedroom window, watching the rising gale sway the hemlock trees in the garden next door. The sky was clear, the moon shaped like the peak of a cap. Glowing fluorescently, sending its cool light over the landscape.

She pulled her satin robe more tightly around herself, shivering as if she were out in the stormy night. She couldn't get Arabella's face out of her mind, the disappointment she couldn't hide when her aunt Lauren had said, "Not tonight, I'm afraid. Could you put it back where you found it? Perhaps you can watch it some other time."

She had spoken too swiftly. It had been her automatic reaction to seeing the label. She had left the video behind when she walked out of her marriage. She had left behind all the things she couldn't bear to look at any more.

She wondered if Zack ever watched the video. Watched the succession of joyful parties caught on film. Becky when she turned one, with her beaming smile showing her first teeth. Then two, when her dark hair had been long enough to swirl on her head. At three, she'd posed in her first ballet tutu. And at four, she'd swum across the pool without her water wings.

Lauren shivered again and was about to turn and go

to bed when she saw the headlights of a car turn into the drive. She recognized the lines of Ben's Lotus.

The car drew to a halt, and Zack got out awkwardly with his crutches.

He gave a salute to whomever was in the car, and it drove off.

Then, taking her by surprise, he glanced at her window.

She knew he saw her. It was too late to draw back.

He gestured to her to come down.

And then he disappeared.

Like a lemming to the sea, she made for the door.

"I told you," he said as she came down the stairs, "not to wait up."

"I didn't. I...couldn't sleep."

"Problem?" He took off his jacket, threw it over a chair. "Everything okay?"

"Oh, yes, everything's fine."

"So." He swung forward. "What kept you awake?"

"Can I get you a nightcap?"

"How about some hot chocolate?"

"I'll bring it into the den."

She hurried away from him and heard him make his way to the den. Her heart felt as if someone were twisting it around and driving spikes into it. He was just so damned attractive. The gale had whipped his hair into strands, and his cheeks were flushed. With the wind? Or had the ruddy color been caused by Scotch?

She heated two mugs of milk in the microwave and added hot chocolate powder, stirring till it dissolved and the tiny marshmallows floated in the froth.

Then she carried the mugs to the den.

Zack was standing at the window, the curtains pulled back, and he was staring at the stars.

"There they are," he murmured, "the Seven Sisters."

"Here." Lauren's voice was a little sharp. "Come and sit down."

She set the mugs on the low round coffee table in front of the hearth. This was the one room in the house where they still burned a wood fire, and though it had been alight earlier, nothing remained but a few glowing embers.

She took some kindling and logs from the brass box to one side of the hearth and soon had the flames jumping merrily up the chimney's throat. She replaced the guard, and when she turned, it was to find Zack sprawled on the couch facing the fire. He patted the cushion next to his.

"Sit here."

They had always sat there together in this room. Feeling helpless to resist, she took her place beside him and reached for her mug.

They sat without talking for a few minutes, the gale outside almost drowning out the spark and crackle of the alder wood and the loud ticking of the antique clock on the mantel. Zack was first to speak.

"I've been thinking," he said, "about you."

"About what, in particular?"

"About your odd remark last night concerning Patsy's perfume. I puzzled over that, but it didn't dawn on me till tonight that you were jealous."

"She's married, Zack!"

"Yeah, but you didn't know that then. You thought there was something going on between us."

She made a sound of protest, but he ignored it.

"And it occurred to me that Arabella might have repeated something I said to her."

"What on earth could that have been!"

"She asked me if I thought Patsy was pretty."

"And you said yes." Lauren tried to sound indifferent. "So...she *is* pretty. Very pretty."

"Did Arabella happen to tell you what I said next?"

Lauren lifted her shoulders in what she hoped looked like a casual shrug. "I don't think so."

"I agreed Patsy was pretty, but that as far as I was concerned the prettiest lady in the whole world was her aunt Lauren." Zack leaned forward and put down his mug. Then he took hers from her unresisting fingers. "Lauren, when I proposed to you, I told you you were the only one for me. I meant it then, with all my heart, and I mean it now."

"It's not you, Zack." Lauren pulled away from him. "It's me."

He heaved out a sigh. "It's Arabella, isn't it? Honey, I think you know it wasn't a setup last night at the Macinaws. But I talked to Jerry today, and he told me about losing their baby. I know it's been tough, but... Can't you see? Bettina suffered, too, but she was able to—"

Lauren got to her feet. "Zack, Bettina's situation was entirely different from mine." She heard her voice shake. Her hands shook, too. She twined them together and pressed them to her stomach as she felt the muscles knot. "It wasn't her fault that she lost her baby."

"For God's sake, Lauren." Grabbing his crutches, Zack lurched from the couch. "It wasn't your fault Becky died!"

She stared at him and could see nothing for her tears.

"I was driving the car," she said. "I was the one driving the car."

CHAPTER NINE

ZACK thundered, "It was an accident, for God's sake!"

"Please don't shout at me."

Tension throbbed in the air between them. He clenched his fists, tried to steady the furious hammering of his heart.

He took in a deep breath, let it out in a rush.

"Sweetheart." His eyes were pleading. "You know it was an accident. The guy ran a red light—"

"I know. I know that." Her lower lip quivered. "But I keep asking myself why I chose that route. Normally, when I drove Becky to her ballet class, I always went along Burrard and down—"

He pressed a firm fingertip to her mouth. "Don't do this to yourself, Lauren. You were in no way to blame for what happened. You were driving well within the speed limit, the lights were in your favor, that teenager barreled through the intersection like a bat out of hell—"

"Zack, I know. Logically, I know I wasn't at fault. But I can't help thinking if only. If only I hadn't gone that way...."

He put his arms around her and held her tight. She was shaking. "I hate to see you so unhappy." He cupped her head against his chest, rested his chin on her crown. "I'd do anything to—"

Choking back a sob, she pulled away from him. "It'll never go away, Zack. The regret. It'll never go away."

"Then," he said quietly, "you're going to have to learn to live with it."

"I'm trying." Her eyes were full of tears. "I am...." She pressed her fingertips to her eyes, brushed away the moisture. "Zack, I'm going to my room now."

He sensed further sympathy was the last thing she needed at this moment. He cleared his throat, deliberately changed the subject, deliberately spoke in a neutral tone.

"I won't see much of you the next couple of days. Tomorrow I'm busy again with the Japanese contingent and at night I have a meeting to attend. Thursday— Christmas Eve—I'll be interviewing the last two nannies on the list, and in the afternoon there'll be the usual party for the staff. I'll be home around, I guess, five-thirty...with the puppy."

She smiled, but it was obviously with an effort. "Arabella's going to be thrilled. You're so good to her, Zack."

"I'd be good to you—" his voice was almost a growl "—if you'd let me."

"I know." She put a hand to his cheek, rested it gently for a moment. "I wish..." She sighed, and with a wistful smile, dropped her hand and turned away. She bent to lift her mug from the coffee table and looked at him again. "Good night, Zack."

"Good night, sweetheart."

He saw the pain in her eyes. He felt the pain in her heart. He watched her leave.

He wanted to go after her. He ached to help her.

But he knew, deep in his soul, that if Lauren were ever to conquer her demons, she would have to do it on her own.

*   *   *

"What's *in* here, Aunt Lauren?"

Lauren was polishing the TV armoire. She paused, yellow duster in hand, and threw Arabella a teasing smile. "That would be telling!"

The day before Christmas and the child had been beside herself with excitement all morning. If she'd rearranged the parcels under the tree once, she'd rearranged them a hundred times. And now she'd taken to shaking them at her ear, trying to guess what was under the wrapping paper.

"I think," she said thoughtfully as she turned a small package over, "this might be a box of felt markers!"

"You do?" Lauren faked a wide, innocent look.

"And this—" Arabella hefted a heavy flat package wrapped in red and decorated with a silver bow and a tiny tinkling silver bell "—has to be a book." She put it down and poked a finger into a loosely wrapped bulky parcel. "This is for Uncle Zack, from you."

As Arabella rummaged through the other packages, Lauren pictured the gift she'd bought for Zack—a fine cashmere robe, belted and thigh-length, in the exact same shade of gray as his eyes. Soft and luxurious, it would, she knew, look very sexy on him. She bit her lip as she was suddenly assailed by doubt. Should she have bought him something less personal? She sighed. It was too late now.

"I guess," Arabella murmured, "Uncle Zack isn't into buying presents."

"What makes you say that?" Lauren spoke in a casual tone. She didn't want to give Arabella any hint that Zack had a very special surprise for her.

"Well, the red velvet cape for Great-Aunt Dolly—it's from you and Uncle Zack, it's got both your names on it, but you were the one who bought it. And all my presents here—well, they've got your writing on the card, from Uncle Zack and Aunt Lauren. But there's nothing here for you. Nothing from Uncle Zack, I mean.''

"Perhaps he's going to pop a present under the tree when he gets home.''

But she wasn't expecting anything. Truth was, she didn't need anything. When their marriage had broken up, Zack had not only bought her the condo, he'd transferred enough money into her bank account to last her a lifetime.

Besides, he'd told her he didn't want her to buy him a present. He obviously meant that to work both ways.

She shouldn't feel disappointed.

Yet, contrarily, she did.

"It's twelve o'clock!'' Dolly's abrasive voice came from the open doorway. "Why isn't lunch on the table?''

Lauren turned irritably, just barely managing to squash back a snappy retort. "I was just about to call you. And I shall be serving it in the kitchen.''

"Why aren't we eating in the dining room?'' Dolly's black eyes sparked indignantly.

"Because I've already set the table there for our evening meal. If you don't want to eat in the kitchen, I'd be happy to bring you a tray in the sitting room.''

"Of course I don't want to eat in the kitchen!'' Dolly whirled. "Bring me that tray, girl, and don't keep me waiting!''

Silence followed her testy departure.

Arabella scrambled to her feet.

"I'll get my hands washed, Aunt Lauren.''

Lauren had made tomato soup for lunch, along with salmon and celery sandwiches and crème caramel for dessert.

She stuck an ivory winter rose in a dainty crystal vase and set it on Dolly's tray. Then she carried the tray from the kitchen. She could hear Arabella in the powder room, and as she passed the half-open door, she heard the child talking to herself.

Amused, she paused and listened.

"And I just hope that Uncle Zack can find me a nanny today "cause if he doesn't, we haven't a hope in heck of winning our case. And if we don't win our case, I'm going to be stuck with Great-Aunt Dolly, and she just plain can't stand me. Well, I don't think it's only me, she just can't stand anybody. Aunt Lauren likes me. A lot. I just know that as sure as sure. But she's not into families any more, because of Becky, so I'm not even letting myself hope that she would want to be my mom."

The sound of water gurgling down the sink made Lauren start. She blinked, and realized tears were spilling down her cheeks. Oh, damn…

She walked quickly to the front hall, set the tray on a rosewood table, took a tissue from her pocket and wiped her eyes. They were red-rimmed, she saw in the oval mirror above the table, and her face was pale and blotchy.

Jaw tightly clenched, she picked up the tray and walked into the sitting room.

"Here's your tray, Dolly."

Dolly Smith shoved her knitting aside. "And about time, too!"

Lauren set the tray on the coffee table with a thump

that almost made the soup spill over. Setting her fists on her hips, she glared at the fractious old woman.

"That's it!" she snapped. "I've had enough of you. You weren't invited to come here. You're making things miserable for everybody around you! Well, I tell you one thing—no more! You smarten up or you can pack and go home. Zack's too polite to turn you out, but I sure as hell am not! So—"

With a guttural sob, she broke off, her anger all at once dissolved in a wail of misery. Hiding her face in her hands, she stumbled away, trying in vain to stop the tidal wave of salty tears. The sounds she was making were ugly, racking, like a wounded animal might make.

She thought she heard Dolly's voice.

She ignored it.

She ran to the stairs, ran up them desperately, aiming for the shelter of her room.

When she reached it, she slammed the door, felt clumsily for the key, turned it in the lock.

She almost fell across the room and threw herself onto the bed.

It was too much for her. It was really too much. She couldn't take it any more.

The pressure from Zack, from Arabella, from Dolly.

All she wanted to do was run away.

"Lauren?"

Zack's voice came from far away. Echoing around and around. As if in a dream.

She came awake groggily, her eyes sticky, her body stiff. The room was in darkness. She lay still, listening.

It came again. His voice.

"Lauren? Are you okay?"

No dream, then, but reality. He was tapping lightly but with increasing urgency on her bedroom door.

She pushed herself up on one elbow. "I'm...fine." She shoved her hair back. It was damp from her tears.

"May I come in?"

Her gaze fell to the bedside clock. It was twenty to six. She'd been asleep for more than five hours.

"No." She sat up, hugged her arms around her knees, stared through the shadows to the door. "I'll...come down."

"Dinner's ready," he said. He gave the door another rat-tat, and then she heard him leave.

She pushed herself off the bed and went to the bathroom. Shivering, she stared at herself in the mirror. What a sight. She looked even worse than she had earlier. Her face was ashen, and her eyes had a bright, wild look that frightened her. And her hair was a tangled mess.

She stripped off her clothes, turned on the shower.

She had planned a lovely Christmas Eve dinner.

Arabella and Zack had been looking forward to it so much.

She had let them down. She had let her emotions get away from her, and she had let them down.

Her mouth twisted in a bitter smile. She had accused Dolly Smith of ruining their Christmas.

She was making a darned good job of doing that all by herself.

Zack raked a distraught hand through his hair as he paced the foyer and waited for Lauren to come downstairs.

What the hell had happened while he was at work? He'd come home early to find a very subdued Arabella drying dishes in the kitchen and an uncharacteristically quiet Dolly Smith working at the counter. Good smells emanated from the oven. One of Lauren's aprons was fastened around the woman's gaunt figure. He'd asked her what was going on, but it was Arabella who had answered.

"Aunt Lauren's upstairs resting. She's not to be disturbed," she'd said somberly.

"Dolly, what in the name of—"

The beady black eyes had been strangely evasive. "She's resting, like the child said. Leave her be."

So he had.

Until Dolly had announced the meal was ready and asked him to summon Lauren.

"Zack?"

He spun at sound of the wavery voice. And felt as if someone had punched him in the gut. Lauren looked awful. Her face was drawn, her eyes strained. Her hair was scraped back, as usual, making her features look stark and sharp. She was wearing a red knit dress that accentuated the red rims around her eyes.

"You've been crying."

She brushed a hand through the air as if swiping away an insect. "I...it was nothing. I guess I was tired. I'm fine now. Really." She glanced toward the kitchen. "Who cooked dinner?"

Whatever was wrong, she obviously didn't want to talk about it. Since that was her prerogative, he decided not to risk upsetting her by pushing the issue.

"Dolly's apparently been in the kitchen all afternoon."

"Dolly?"

Arabella called from the dining-room doorway, "Dinner's ready, everybody!"

They moved together across the foyer.

"Zack," Lauren whispered, "what about the puppy? Did you get him?"

"I snuck him in earlier. He's tucked away in his new basket with a hot water bottle and an alarm clock in my room."

"What about the nannies? Any luck?"

He shook his head. "Back to square one," he said. "But I'll worry about that after Christmas."

Dolly had baked the ham Lauren had planned for the evening meal, and had given it a festive look with pineapple rings and cherries. She served it, on heated plates, with delicious scalloped potatoes, a green bean casserole and a fabulous turnip soufflé. For dessert, she brought in a steamed syrup sponge and a jug of thin sweet custard that tasted like ambrosia.

The meal was a quiet one, with a certain tension in the air. Dolly insisted on doing all the serving, but otherwise spoke not a word.

Arabella asked to be excused after dessert.

"Sure," Lauren said. "But run up and clean your teeth before you do anything else. Syrup tends to stick."

After she'd gone, Dolly brought coffee, but instead of sitting down after she poured it, she announced that she was going to drink hers in the sitting room.

"Shall I carry your cup for you?" Lauren asked, looking directly at Dolly for the first time since their fight at lunchtime. She felt a jolt of dismay when she saw how haggard the elderly woman looked. Her black eyes were dull, and her jowls hung loosely, as if she no longer had the strength or will to keep her muscles taut.

"Thank you." Dolly's voice was oddly hollow. "I can manage."

Zack got to his feet. "Dolly, that was one terrific dinner."

"It was," Lauren agreed. "I don't know when I last had such a superbly cooked meal."

Dolly whisked an enormous white handkerchief from her bag and blew her nose, the sound loud as a foghorn and just as penetrating. "It has been brought to my attention," she said stiffly to Zack, "that I am unwanted here. I shall pack my bags in the morning and be on my way. I have been here long enough to see how the wind's blowing."

Stunned, Lauren stared at her. Zack seemed equally flabbergasted at this turn of events.

"But you can't go!" he said. "At least, not tomorrow! For heaven's sake, it's Christmas Day!"

"He's right, Dolly," Lauren murmured. "Besides, you'll never get a seat on a plane at such short notice."

"With Zack's connections, that should be no problem. Besides, most people don't travel on Christmas Day. The planes will be empty."

If Lauren hadn't already noticed how haggard Dolly looked, she might not have noticed the quaver in a voice that was usually harsh and cold. She felt a surge of compassion. She should be glad Dolly was leaving, glad for Zack's sake and for Arabella's, too. But somehow she wasn't.

She watched, vexedly, as Dolly swept from the room. Then she turned to Zack, who had slumped in his seat.

"You know something?" His grin was wry. "I'd just begun to get used to the old bat!"

"Zack, it's my fault. We had a row at lunchtime, and I...well, I totally lost it! Told her where to go. That's why she's leaving. I feel really badly about it."

"It was bound to happen," he said. "If it hadn't been you, it would've been me. She was starting to drive me nuts."

"She seems determined to go. But will you be able to get her a flight tomorrow?"

"I'll try. I'd better get onto it right now, though."

"What she said—about seeing how the wind was blowing—what do you think she meant?"

"Oh, that's pretty obvious," he said dryly. "She knows the score with us, knows we aren't getting back together. And she knows I haven't found a nanny." He shrugged. "She'll go ahead and sue for custody of Arabella."

Lauren sighed. "It's a mess, isn't it? What—"

"Uncle Zack! Aunt Lauren!" Arabella's shrill voice screamed their names, and they hurried into the foyer.

The little girl was running down the stairs, her red hair streaming like a glorious banner behind her, her eyes shining with joy, her cheeks flushed so pink they glowed.

And in her arms was a black and white bundle of fur. Fur with a shrimp-pink nose and inquisitive brown eyes and four white paws sticking up in the air.

"Just look what I found upstairs!" she cried. "I went into Uncle Zack's bathroom to look for some toothpaste 'cause mine was finished, and he—" she hugged the pup so tight he gave a squeaky bark "—was sitting up in a basket! What was he doing there, Uncle Zack?"

Breathlessly, she stared at him, her lips parted, her whole body rigid with tension.

Zack chuckled. "What do you think he was doing there, pumpkin? Why, he was waiting for you, of course!"

"He's *mine?*" Arabella's eyes were wide as plates.

"He's all yours, sweetie."

"Oh, Uncle Zack!" The child looked at him adoringly. "And can I be the one to pick his name?"

"Sure you can. So, what's it going to be?"

"I don't know. I'll have to think about it." Arabella cuddled the dog, her smile one of blissful contentment, then tilted her face to Zack again. "Why didn't you put him under the tree?"

"Well, we all know what pups do when they're around trees, don't we!"

Arabella giggled. "We know that, all right! I'm gonna have to walk him a lot. Did you buy him a lead?"

"Yeah, you'll find it upstairs in my bedroom, on the dresser. Why don't you go get it and we'll take what's-his-name for a walk in the back yard."

Arabella took off up the stairs, and Lauren walked to the hall closet. As she opened the door and slipped Arabella's jacket from its hanger, she heard the wind howling around the front of the house.

"It's quite a night." She closed the closet door and walked to Zack.

"Lauren." He touched her arm. "I have a Christmas gift for you. I'll give you it after Arabella and Dolly have gone to bed."

"You didn't have to-"

"I wanted to."

Arabella came downstairs, and Lauren was left wondering what on earth he had bought her.

It turned out that Zack's Christmas gift was not on earth.

But it was several hours before he finally told her where it was—and what it was!

He and Lauren had spent the evening in the den, with the fire leaping cozily and Arabella crawling gleefully around the carpet after the pup, whose energy was surpassed only by her own.

Dolly—who had turned down Zack's invitation to join them in the den—went to bed shortly after nine. The pup had conked out by that time, and Lauren allowed Arabella to stay up late, watching a children's Christmas movie.

It had been agreed that tonight the puppy would sleep in Zack's bathroom, where Zack had already spread out layers of newspapers to allow for accidents.

"You can start training him tomorrow," he said to Arabella as Lauren tucked the child into bed. "He'll have to learn to do his business first thing every morning, and you'll have to take him out at a regular time."

"I can do that," she promised, and then, a small frown pleating her brow, she said, "Uncle Zack, what's gonna happen if we don't win our case? Great-Aunt Dolly doesn't like dogs, and her apartment is so teensy there wouldn't even be room for one."

"The pup is yours," Zack said. "Whatever happens. Worse comes to worst, you'll spend some of your holidays here. The pooch won't forget you. Heck, dogs have better memories than elephants!"

"Pooch. I like that," she murmured over a yawn. "That's what I'm gonna call my pup. Poochie." She snuggled down, and her eyes drifted shut. "Night, Aunt Lauren. Night, Uncle Zack."

She was asleep, Lauren was sure, before they left the room.

As she and Zack made their way downstairs, she said, "Would you like a mug of eggnog?"

"Lots of rum in it?"

Her eyes twinkled. "Enough!"

"You've twisted my arm."

As Zack waited in the den for Lauren, he stood at the window and looked at the heavens. The sky was clear, the stars winking like diamonds, the quarter moon crisply defined.

In the Fleetwoods' driveway something clattered—a garbage can whirled by the wind? In the garden adjoining Lindenlea to the east, tall trees swayed violently, their trunks creaking, their branches flailing in the wintry blast. Hemlocks, he reflected, frowning. Damned dangerous, with those shallow roots, so easily ripped out of the soil. The trees should have been cut down years ago, but the landlord was an absentee one and—

"Here we are!"

He turned and saw Lauren come into the den and shoulder the door shut. She was carrying their drinks along with a plate of savoury-smelling hors d'oeuvres on a silver tray.

"Lauren," he said as she set the tray on the coffee table, "I want to give you your present."

"Me first." She straightened and touched her topknot with what looked like a nervous gesture. The red knit dress touched her in all the right places, places where he wanted to touch her, too. "Just a sec."

She crossed to the tree and crouched.

When she got up, she was holding a bulky package wrapped in shiny silver and cobalt blue paper, decorated with a fancy gold and silver bow.

Her cheeks were pink.

"Don't...read anything into this." She sounded flustered. "It was—well, I..."

"Why don't I just open it," he said, amused, and took the present.

He didn't sit down, but stood leaning on his crutches as he untied the ribbons and opened the parcel.

"Ah!" He opened the gray cashmere robe and whistled. "This sure is nice. How did you know my old one was getting frayed?" He adopted a mock scowl. "Have you been poking around in my room?"

"No, of course not!"

"Just kidding!" He tucked the robe into the box and dropped the box on the chair by his side. "Come here."

Her cheeks became even pinker. She didn't move.

"Come here," he growled. "I'm not going to eat you!"

Like a shy child, she came forward.

"Closer."

She took another two steps. Which brought her close enough. He leaned forward and kissed her on the brow.

"Thanks," he said. "I love it."

She was wearing the challenging perfume. The one that had turned him off the first time he'd smelled it, in the elevator. Now it turned him on. Oh, boy, did it ever turn him on! But her skin looked so tightly drawn, her movements so jerky and her body so tense, he knew this was not the moment for the kind of kiss he desperately wanted to give her.

"I'm glad you like it. When I saw it—" she hugged her arms around herself "—it made me think of you."

"Yeah." He forced a light chuckle. "Gray and soft, like a mouse."

She gave a half-laugh, but it seemed to catch in her throat. "A mouse," she said huskily, "you are not!"

He turned and swung over to the window. "Come see," he said quietly, "what I bought for you."

Bewildered, arms still wrapped around herself, Lauren crossed to stand beside him. He was looking at the sky.

She followed his gaze.

"See them?" he asked. "The Pleiades? The Seven Sisters?"

For a moment she couldn't speak, then she said, over the lump in her throat, "Alcyone, Electra, Merope, Taygete, Celaeno, Sterope—"

"And Maia," he finished softly.

"Maia. According to myth, the firstborn and the most beautiful of all the Sisters."

"And some say the brightest. Brighter even than Alcyone."

She looked at him, her eyes misted with memories.

"Sweetheart, I know how you love to look at the stars. And I know that when you do, you think of Becky. That star, Maia, that bright and most beautiful little star..." He reached behind the curtains and brought out a picture.

No, not a picture. A framed star map. With a printed declaration. But what was this all about?

"Remember on Monday," he said, "when you came into my study while I was on the phone? I knew I hurt you by asking you to leave. But the reason I did was I was talking to the people at the space center and I didn't want you to overhear.''

He held out the declaration, and after the briefest of hesitations, she took it.

She began to read, and felt the skin at her nape prickle faintly, as if a small ghost were looking over her shoulder, spelling out the words and whispering them along with her.

This certifies that Lauren and Zack Alexander have named a star in the constellation Taurus and that from the date of December 25, this star will be registered at the Pacific Space Centre, Vancouver, Canada by the name, Rebecca Alexander.

A star? A star for Becky?

''I heard about this deal the space center has.'' Zack's voice was gentle. ''They sell local rights to any of the unclaimed stars in the heavens. It's a fund-raiser for the space center. From now on, when you look into the night sky, perhaps seeing Becky's star with six sisters clustered around her will give you a feeling of...comfort.''

''Oh, Zack.'' Gulping back a sob, Lauren put her arms around him and hid her face against his chest. ''What a wonderful thing to do....''

''Hey, I didn't want you to cry.'' He tipped her chin up. ''I wanted it to make you happy.''

She smiled through her tears. ''I am, Zack.''

Again, he wanted to kiss her. Kiss her on those trembling lips. But she looked so fragile and vulnerable. It would be taking advantage. And she was having a rough enough time without him putting any extra pressure on her.

So he sat with her on the sofa, and they drank their eggnog and ate the snacks set out on the china plate.

And when they were finished, she carried the tray to the kitchen. He waited for her at the foot of the stairs. They went up together, and before they went their separate ways, they wished each other a merry Christmas, because it had just turned twelve o'clock.

CHAPTER TEN

LAUREN couldn't sleep.

It wasn't surprising, of course, since she'd slept all afternoon, and in the end, she gave up trying.

She put on her robe and went downstairs. The fire had gone out in the den, and she wandered to the kitchen, where she poured herself a tot of brandy, thinking it might make her drowsy.

Cupping the delicate balloon glass in both hands, she went to the den. She switched on the light, crossed to the TV and switched it on.

She was about to sit down again when she saw, on the bookshelf beside the TV armoire, the video Arabella had asked her to play.

Becky's birthday video.

It should have been put back with the other videos, in the wide storage area of the armoire, behind closed doors.

She put down her glass, scooped up the video and crossed to the armoire. She crouched to open the doors and tuck the video away...but found herself stopping, video in one hand, shiny brass knob in the other.

She wanted to put the video away, wanted to push it out of sight. Out of sight, out of mind.

But something welled up inside her, something powerful and frightening and demanding. Something stronger than her physical self, something that wouldn't be denied.

An inner compulsion drove her to close the door. Forced her to her feet. And made her slide the video into the empty maw of the VCR.

As if on automatic pilot, she pressed the buttons to start the movie, used the tracking button to get a perfect picture, turned the sound up loud enough so she could hear it but not so loud it would disturb those sleeping upstairs. And then, walking backward like a wound-up robot, stumbled to the sofa.

She lowered herself onto the soft cushions, blindly swept out a hand to grab a pillow, and sitting forward, pillow clutched to her chest, she stared at the set.

It was like an agonizing blow to the heart when Becky's image flashed on the screen. She winced, grabbed the pillow tighter, fought the desperate urge to lurch up and switch the TV off. Why was she doing this? Until now, she had deliberately, determinedly, fiercely avoided looking at anything that would remind her of Becky and tear open all the old scars.

But it was as if she was hypnotized.

She couldn't move.

She couldn't drag her eyes away.

She stared, oblivious of the world around her, while the scenes played out for her, scenes that were so joyful, so heartbreakingly happy and full of warmth, she thought she couldn't bear it.

Till this night, she hadn't been able to bear even the thought of doing this. Not even the thought of it.

But now she watched, still as a frozen statue, while the reel played through from her daughter's very first birthday till the day of her last. Till the day of her fourth birthday.

Becky swimming. A scorchingly hot day. Four of her little friends in the pool with her.

Arabella was one of those friends.

Mac and Lisa had come up from L.A. for a week. The girls hadn't seen each other for a year, but it was as if they'd never parted. They were inseparable.

Becky in a scarlet and white striped bikini, Arabella in a cream one-piece. They played and swam and shrieked and ate and—

There. The very last shot.

Becky and Arabella mugging for the camera after everyone else had gone home. Arms around each other, heads close, faces beaming…

And…fade out.

The VCR continued to run, black and white speckles, the faintest hum of sound.

How long she sat there, Lauren didn't know. She didn't know she'd been crying till she finally slackened her grip on the cushion and realized it was soaked.

Soaked with her tears.

She sank against the sofa back, feeling absolutely drained of emotion. As if she'd been swimming against the tide for years, and it had turned at last, and after its tumultuous punishing pounding, finally tossed her onto the beach. Safe. Battered but safe.

She slipped down the knit cuffs of her robe and used them to wipe her eyes. Her breath had a labored quality, and the skin on her back was coated with sweat.

But her heart felt light. Lighter than she had thought it could ever feel again.

She got up and switched off the TV, set the VCR to rewind.

While it did, she crossed to the window.

The gale was still blowing savagely, and in the distance she heard the sound of sirens.

She raised her gaze to the clear heavens.

Looked at Becky's star.

"Merry Christmas," she whispered. "Merry Christmas, my darling daughter."

The star twinkled at her.

That special star, the one that was so bright and most beautiful of all.

"Wake up, Aunt Lauren!" Arabella jumped on the bed, rousing her honorary aunt from sleep. "It's Christmas Day!"

Lauren murmured drowsily, half-opened her eyes and through her lashes saw an eager little face almost lost in a cloud of auburn curls.

From way deep down in her heart, she felt a rising surge of emotion. Affection and much, much more.

"Merry Christmas, honey," she said huskily. Reaching out, she pulled Arabella into her arms and gave her a warm hug. To her astonishment, Arabella drew back and stared at her, and then, green eyes suddenly aglisten with tears, she threw her wiry arms around Lauren and hugged her with so much energy and fervor that Lauren was left breathless.

"Merry Christmas, Aunt Lauren!" Cheeks flushed pink, Arabella pulled down her sweater. "Sorry if I wakened you, but it's gone eight—"

"Gone eight?" Her curiosity about Arabella's odd reaction forgotten in the horror of the moment, Lauren shot to a sitting position. "Hell's teeth—Dolly!" But before she could get out of bed, Arabella spoke quickly.

"It's okay. Uncle Zack was up early, and he looked

after Great-Aunt Dolly. She's had her breakfast—her hot strong tea and her hot buttered toast!'' Arabella's wide grin let Lauren know Arabella was fully aware of, and amused by, the elderly woman's fussiness. ''And me'n Uncle Zack are going to take Poochie into the garden for a walk.''

''Ah, Poochie.'' Lauren ran a hand over the bouncy auburn hair of this adorable child. Arabella. Tender and feminine one minute, bouncy and tomboyish the next. But at all times open and honest, never afraid to show her need for love, and in the process exposing herself to the inevitable hurts and reflections but bravely soldiering on in spite of them. ''Did the pup behave last night?''

Arabella grimaced. ''Not *that* well.''

Lauren laughed. ''He'll learn.''

''Yup. That's what Uncle Zack said.'' Arabella jumped off the bed. ''Gotta go, he's probably waiting for me. Will you be down soon?''

''I'm getting up now.'' Lauren stretched and watched lazily as Arabella flew from the room.

What a deep sleep she had been in. Deep and dreamless. She felt wonderfully rested and relaxed, and filled to overflowing with joy and a blissful sense of anticipation.

Smiling, she got up and wandered to the window.

She pulled back the curtains and saw that though it was a bright day—sunny, blue-skied and cloudless—it was very windy. The gale had abated somewhat, but the wind still rushed fiercely over the garden, rippling the leafy tops of the giant rhododendron bushes, waving the branches of the hemlock trees in the next yard.

She was about to turn away when she saw Zack and Arabella appear. They were both in parkas and jeans,

Zack with his crutches, manipulating them now with suck ease, and Arabella tightly holding a blue lead with Poochie straining ahead of her.

Lauren put the flat of her hands against the cool panes and looked at them. Zack, whom she had always loved and would never stop loving. And Arabella, whom she had tried not to love and had found it impossible.

Tears sprang to her eyes. Zack and Arabella. They were her family. How could she have denied it to herself? She should have known it from the beginning, should have known it from the moment Tyler Braddock had told them she and Zack had become guardians to the child.

Zack had told her she had to let go. Let go of Becky.

And she had. She finally had. She wasn't sure of the exact moment it had happened. It might have been when Zack had shown her Becky's star, or it might have been when she'd watched the birthday video. But it didn't really matter. What mattered was that she had come to terms, at last, with Becky's death.

She would never get over her loss, but she would carry it with her, gently, into the future.

And she was ready, now, to face that future head-on.

She couldn't wait to tell Zack. She knew he'd be over the moon. A family was all he'd ever wanted. And of course it was all Arabella wanted, too...but Zack would be the first to know. The first to know they would be husband and wife again, a couple in every sense of the word.

A gust of wind whistled around the house, the piercing sound tugging her thoughts from their suddenly sensual path. Time to have a shower, time to get dressed.

Eyes still dreamy, her lips curved in a soft smile, she glanced into the garden as she started to turn away—

And froze.

No! It couldn't be!

But it was.

One of the ancient hemlock trees next door had been uprooted by the gale and was falling, a giant bent on destruction, into Lindenlea's back garden.

In the fleeting shock-filled moment before she lurched into action, the scene exploded in Lauren's mind like something from a hellish nightmare.

Arabella, clutching Poochie's lead, watching the pup as he excitedly sniffed around an azalea bush at the bottom of the garden.

Zack, adding birdseed to the wooden feeder suspended from the apple tree outside the window.

He had his back to Arabella.

And Arabella was directly in the path of the falling tree.

Lauren screamed, a shrill scream of terror. She grabbed the window. She couldn't get it up. She battered on the glass, screaming all the time. "Arabella! Arabella!" But the child continued to stand where she was, her indulgent gaze on the dog, while Zack—

Zack had turned. Had seen. His face a picture of horror, he shouted. She saw his lips move. He headed towards the child faster than he'd ever moved...but he wasn't going to make it. It wasn't humanly possible for him to get there in time.

Lauren spun and raced for the door, sobs rasping in her throat, her heart pumping so hard it might burst.

Dolly's bedroom door burst open as she passed it.

"What's the matter, girl?"

"Call emergency!" Lauren leaped down the stairs. "Get an ambulance here and a firetruck and tell them to hurry!"

Her bare feet skimmed like cold pebbles across the corridor as she made for the kitchen door, and when she opened the door the wind lashed her with icy whips. Fear lashed her heart with whips even colder when she saw Zack violently dragging aside branches of the fallen tree.

Under there, somewhere, was Arabella.

Lauren stumbled over trunk and branches and felt her soul cry out in sorrow when she at last reached Zack and saw that he had found his little charge.

She was lying on her side, her auburn hair bright against the winter-browned lawn and green hemlock needles. Her eyes were closed, her face was the color of fresh snow, and the blood on her brow was red as holly berries.

Poochie was crouched nearby, whimpering, held fast in place by his lead, which was tangled around a branch.

In the distance, Lauren heard the sound of a siren.

"Zack—"

"I don't want to move her." Zack's voice was clotted with tears. Eyes fixed on Arabella, he touched her white cheek. "I daren't, in case…"

"It's all right," she whispered as she crouched beside him. "The ambulance is on its way."

The waiting room was so damned small!

No room to pace—not that he could pace with these confounded crutches.

Zack thumped onto one of the three vinyl-covered chairs, closed his eyes and sent up another prayer.

Dear God, let her live.

He said the words over and over and over in his head.

He couldn't say them aloud.

He knew he would break down.

And Lauren needed him to be strong.

He opened his eyes—the lids felt like lead—and looked at her.

She was sitting across from him, slumped on the low chair with the slack-limbed posture of a puppet. Only her hands were taut, steepled under her chin as if she was praying. Her face was pale, the skin over her nose and cheeks pulled tight. And her eyes, as she stared into space, were blank.

His fear for Arabella swelled to encompass his wife.

"Lauren?"

She stirred, and after a long moment slowly shifted her gaze to him. "Why—" her voice was a mere whisper "—are they taking so long?"

"Tests. More X rays. They're giving her the works."

"No bones broken, just minor scrapes and bruises, the specialist said. Except for...her head."

Swallowing hard, Zack got up and swung to the doorway. He looked both ways. No one was coming.

He stood with his back to the waiting room. Stared unseeingly at the pastel pink wall across the corridor. If only... If only he'd been watching. If only he'd walked the pup himself. If only...

He was hardly aware he'd groaned till he heard Lauren come up behind him.

"Zack?"

He leaned against the doorjamb and looked at her despairingly. "I keep blaming myself."

She stared at him. "For what?"

He lifted his wide shoulders in an infinitely weary shrug. "For not taking better care of her."

"Zack!" Her voice trembled with protest. "I don't understand—"

"I should have been watching her. I should have—"

"It wasn't your fault. I can't believe you think it was! You—" She broke off and took his hands urgently in hers "Zack, you're the one who tried to persuade me it wasn't my fault we lost Becky! You are no more to blame for what happened this morning than I was when I drove that car! Don't you *see?*"

She was right, of course. Deep down he knew she was right. But he remembered what she said when he tried to convince her of her own innocence. *The regret will never go away.*

He knew he'd feel the same if Arabella didn't pull through. The regret would never go away. If only he'd done something different...taken Arabella out the front instead of the back, taken her along the street instead of—

She squeezed his hands. "Okay?"

He slid his hands free, wrapped his arms around her and pulled her into his embrace. She was so thin, so fragile. He buried his face in her hair—hair that spilled in a silken tumble, unconfined, as there had been no time to do anything with it in the rush to get to the hospital. She was wearing a cotton sweatshirt and jeans, and she smelled of coffee, the strong black vending machine coffee he had finally gotten her to drink about half an hour ago.

"Sweetheart." He ran shaky hands up and down her back. "I know how hard this is for you."

She hugged him hard. "And for you, Zack."

She felt as if her heart was breaking.

She loved him so much, and she wanted so much to be his wife again. But had she left it too late?

If Arabella didn't pull through, was their marriage forever doomed? Oh, she knew Zack loved her. But could he ever forgive her for having rejected the child's love from the moment of her arrival? It would surely corrode their relationship, spoil what could have been perfect again.

She could tell him, now, that she'd come to terms with the past, that she had at last opened her heart to Arabella and was yearning for the three of them to become a family. But would he believe her? Would he believe she had made the decision hours ago, before the accident happened?

Why should he? She'd given him no reason to believe she might be even close to letting herself love Arabella. If she told him she did love the little girl—love her with all her heart—wouldn't he doubt the sincerity of her statement? Wouldn't he think the timing suspect? How convenient to let herself love the child just when Arabella's life was in the balance!

Despair coiled through her, making her feel even more miserable than she already was. If that were possible.

"Lauren?"

She looked at him, her eyes swimming with tears so his face was blurred. "Mmm?"

"What did you say to Arabella this morning?"

"Say?" She frowned, puzzled. "Why, just...wished her a merry Christmas..."

"And you gave her a big hug."

She nodded, her throat aching painfully. "Yes," she said huskily, "a big hug."

"She told me, when she came downstairs, that you were going to be her new mom after all. She said she knew because you hugged her first. Was she right?"

"Oh, Zack—" was this miracle really happening? "—she was...and I love her so much. But I fought it so hard—"

"Ah, sweetheart, you've made me the happiest man in—"

"Mr. Alexander?"

Lauren's arms jerked convulsively, and she dropped them as she and Zack turned toward the voice.

It was the surgeon. Dark-haired, trim, Asian. Behind his glasses, his eyes gleamed with compassion.

"Arabella," he said quietly, "is in a coma—"

Lauren put her hands to her mouth, felt the scalding hot tears well again. Zack put an arm around her. "Hang on, sweetheart," he said.

"But you can come and see her now," the surgeon added.

They followed him along the silent corridor, followed him through double swing doors and past gurneys half hidden by discreetly placed screens.

Lauren braced herself as he stopped and tugged back a heavy green curtain.

Arabella lay on her back. Her eyes were closed, her auburn lashes feathering the smudged circles under her eyes. Her face was as white as the bandage around her head, her freckles so dark they were almost black. Her lips were pale and dry-looking, her breathing shallow.

Lauren leaned against Zack, and he felt steady as a rock. She struggled against the waves of faintness that threatened to overcome her.

"We'll be moving her shortly into a private room,"

the surgeon said. "If you'd care to go to the waiting room, I'll have someone tell you when she's settled in."

"We can sit with her?" Zack asked.

"Of course," the surgeon said.

"How long do you think the coma will last?" Lauren's voice was tattered at the edges.

The surgeon shook his head. "We have no way of knowing. All you can do now is wait. And pray."

Christmas day passed in a blur. As did Boxing Day, the day after, and the days after that.

Lauren and Zack took turns sitting with Arabella. They made sure she was never alone. And with every passing hour, their anxiety and their sorrow increased. But life had to go on, and both she and Zack had things to do besides waiting and watching at Arabella's bedside.

On the morning of the thirty-first, Zack went in to the office at Alexander Electronics to present the year-end bonuses to his staff. And late that afternoon, while Zack took over his shift at the hospital, Lauren drove to her place of employment in search of Jack Perrini.

She found her boss—immaculately dressed in a sharp gray suit, pink shirt and snazzy polka-dotted bow tie—in the front office. He was sharing cranberry punch and shortbread with the staff, a small party, they explained to Lauren, to celebrate the end of the old year, the advent of the new.

Jack Perrini was a workaholic with thinning brown hair and a lean build. He also had a laid-back manner that was distinctly at odds with the shrewdness in his amber eyes.

Lauren felt those amber eyes dissecting her as she

responded to everyone's warm welcome. She declined a glass of punch, and when she whispered to Jack that she wanted a word alone with him he ushered her into his office.

And shut the door.

He waited till she'd sat on the chair in front of his desk before hitching his hip on the edge of the desk.

He frowned at her.

"What the hell's wrong?" he growled. "You look like death warmed up! I gave you a holiday for God's sake! Where did you spend it? The salt mines of Siberia?"

Lauren clasped her hands tightly on top of her bag on her lap. "That might have been more fun," she said.

"More fun than what?"

She filled her employer in on everything that had occurred in her life in the past two weeks.

His eyes gleamed with compassion as he listened to the tale. "So," he said, "the poor kid's still on the danger list. God, what a hell of a thing to happen."

"What I've really come to tell you," Lauren plunged on, "is that I'm turning down your offer of a promotion. The Toronto posting. I'm going to be staying here. Permanently. I'm—I've reconciled with my husband. I'm sorry, Jack. I know I'm letting you down on this, but my marriage comes before anything else."

Her boss raised his brows. "Does that mean you're quitting your job altogether?"

"Do you want me to stay on? In this office?"

"Damned right I do!"

She made a restless movement with one hand. "I can't make any decisions right now."

He stood. "I understand. I'm not going to put any pressure on you. But if all goes well with the kid, and once you get her settled in at school, I'd really like to have you back. Even on a part-time basis. Maybe three days a week? Or mornings only. Whichever you'd prefer.''

Lauren stood. "I can't really think about it at the moment—" her voice caught "—but it means a lot to me that you still want me here and you'd take me on part-time.''

Since Arabella's accident, she was very emotional, and tears seemed to hover constantly just under the surface. She felt them well up. Moved by Jack's kindness, she found herself reaching out spontaneously to embrace him and brush a quick kiss over his cheek. "Thanks, Jack.''

She could tell he was surprised. The Lauren he knew was cool and reserved. But after a beat, he gave her an affectionate hug in return.

"Take care," he said gruffly. Putting an arm around her shoulder, he led her to the door. "And keep in touch. You going home now?''

"No, to the hospital. I'll sit with Arabella from now till eleven-thirty, then Zack'll come in and sit with her for the rest of the night.''

"I hope this waiting will soon be over for you," Jack said as he walked her to her car.

"I hope so," Lauren said. And shivered.

"Cold wind," Jack murmured.

She nodded. But she knew it wasn't the cold wind that had been responsible for her involuntary shiver. It was her bone-deep worry about Arabella and the thought of what it might mean when the waiting was finally over.

"Dolly has really turned up trumps," Zack said to Lauren that night when he arrived at the hospital to take his shift. "Helping with the cleaning, answering the telephone, feeding Poochie, doing most of the cooking." He shrugged off his leather jacket and slung it over a chair by the bed.

"She certainly made everything run more smoothly. I've not been able to concentrate on planning meals or doing much else..." Lauren's words trailed away as her troubled gaze drifted to Arabella.

The child lay on her back, her eyes closed, her thin chest rising and falling evenly under the cotton blanket.

Zack lifted one fine-boned hand from the cover, stroked the pale skin gently. "How has she been, sweetheart?"

"The doctor says there's been a faint improvement, but to me—" Lauren sighed wearily "—she looks just the same."

For a long moment there was silence between them, and then Lauren asked, with an attempt to stimulate conversation, "What did Dolly give you for dinner?"

"Oh, some kind of a fancy omelet and green salad. I told her I wasn't hungry, but she insisted."

"She's right when she says that even if we don't have an appetite, we must eat. But now—" Lauren's lips moved in a wan smile "—she considers the kitchen her domain. She won't let me set foot in it when she's around!"

"It's keeping her busy," Zack said. "And is it my imagination or is she really less abrasive since the two of you had that row?"

"She's mellowed quite a bit," Lauren admitted. "And even calls me by my name, now that I've 'come to my senses,' as she put it, and stopped running! She's not so bad, Zack. Set in her ways, of course, but it seems we may have misjudged her. She told me last night that she only sent Arabella to boarding school because she truly thought it would be better for her to be living with children her own age rather than with an elderly spinster. And she arranged for her to have grief counseling at the school, which perhaps explains why Arabella has adjusted so well to her loss.''

"Yeah, she told me about the counseling. Said Arabella responded well.'' Zack glanced at his watch and then frowned. "It's late. You should be going.''

"I've been thinking about that,'' Lauren said quietly. "Zack, I want to stay here. I want to take in the New Year with you. With you…and Arabella.''

"In that case—'' he got to his feet "—I'd better give Dolly a call. I told her you'd be home before midnight.''

"I'm so glad,'' Lauren murmured, "that she's not going to fight us for custody of Arabella. That was the best Christmas present she could have given us.''

Zack touched her shoulder. "She knows Arabella's better off with us, with two parents, especially two who are absolutely crazy about one another—''

"Even though they're still sleeping in separate bedrooms!'' Lauren grimaced. "Zack, are you sure you don't mind about that? I just feel the time isn't right for—''

"Sweetheart,'' he said softly, "I feel the same way. But I warn you, after this is all over, I'm going to take you on a second honeymoon, and we'll make up for all the time we've spent apart.'' He move to the door as a nurse came in. "I'll call Dolly,'' he said. "And be right back.''

Attached to the wall and angled toward the bed was a small portable TV.

Shortly before midnight, Zack switched it on, keeping the volume low. Just before the countdown began, they got to their feet and stood together, looking at Arabella.

"Do you think," Lauren murmured, "that she can hear us when we talk to her?"

"Yeah, it's very possible."

Lauren bit her lip. "I feel kind of selfish leaving Dolly on her own. Do you think I should have gone home—"

Outside the room there was a kerfuffle.

Voices, determined voices. Arguing. The door opened. At the same time, on the TV, the countdown began.

Lauren swung around and almost reeled with shock when she saw Dolly come in the door, resplendent in the crimson velvet cape. In the background, a frazzled-looking nurse threw up her hands as the door was slammed in her face.

"Dolly?" Lauren's gasp almost choked her when she noticed that Dolly was carrying Poochie.

"Idiotic woman!" Dolly's tone was outraged. "Doesn't she know that animals are good therapy for the sick?"

Six, five, four, three, two, one...

Wild cheers came from the TV. Looking as stunned as Lauren felt, Zack took his wife in his arms, said, "Happy New Year, sweetheart," and kissed her.

Then he turned to Dolly. But she had already taken a seat on the other side of the bed and was depositing Poochie on the covers. The pup set his forepaws on Arabella's shoulder. He sniffed her hair with his shrimp-pink nose.

Then he sat back on his little haunches and barked.

The sound was sharp and demanding.

Lauren saw Zack frown and glance quickly at the door before returning his gaze to the bed.

"For Pete's sake," he muttered to Dolly, "do you really think this was a good idea? After all—"

He broke off with an incredulous gasp. And stared at Arabella. As did Dolly. As did Lauren.

The child had stirred. Hadn't she?

"Arabella?" Zack said, disbelieving. Afraid to believe.

Slowly, slowly, the auburn eyelashes fluttered. Slowly, slowly, the eyelids rose.

But even as Lauren watched with a fervent prayer, she felt her heartbeats slip a notch. Arabella's eyes were open…but they were blank as an empty page.

Digging her teeth into her lip, Lauren slumped onto her chair and clutched Arabella's hand. Zack crouched by the chair. His big hand enfolded hers.

"Oh, Zack," she whispered apprehensively.

"Hang on, sweetheart," he murmured. "This is good. She's coming to."

But…was Arabella going to be all right? Had she come through the accident unscathed, or had she, as the doctor had warned might happen, suffered permanent injury to—

Arabella's eyelashes fluttered again. She whimpered, as if she was having a bad dream. Lauren held her breath as she saw the eyelids rise heavily, saw the thin body move a fraction. And she felt the world stand still as she waited. Zack's breathing was ragged. Dolly's agitated.

She felt a leap of hope when she saw that though Arabella's green eyes were unfocused, they were no longer blank. The child seemed to be looking at Zack.

"Honey?" Zack's voice trembled. "Can you—"

Arabella swallowed and ran her tongue over her parched lips. "My head hurts," she whispered. Her gaze drifted from Zack to Lauren.

Lauren thought surely her throat was going to close up completely as it swelled with emotion. "Sweetie?" She leaned forward.

Arabella's eyelids flickered down again.

"Zack!" Lauren's voice caught. "We have to call a nurse."

"Yeah." He put an arm around her and held her hard, painfully hard. "In a minute."

A sigh came from Arabella.

Hardly daring to draw air into her lungs in case she might drown out a sound from the child, Lauren watched as Arabella's eyelids quivered again. Then they rose, so slowly the suspense was almost palpable, till they were open wide. Her gaze was more focused than before.

"Honey," Zack said urgently, "can you see us?"

"Yes, I can see you, Uncle Zack." Her voice was as wispy as thistledown. "And Aunt Lauren."

"Can you see *me*, child?"

A small frown of concentration tugged Arabella's brows as she turned her head. "Yes, Great-Aunt Dolly."

"You've been lying here in the hospital for a whole week, child. Fine thing—" she sniffed "—missing Christmas!"

"I missed *Christmas*?" Arabella asked on a quaver.

"Today's the first day of January." Lauren had been unaware that she was crying till she felt hot tears plop onto her hand. "Happy New Year, Arabella."

She heard Zack clear his throat, and guessed he was as choked up as she was. Dolly had taken out one of her big handkerchiefs and was trumpeting into its white folds.

"Is this a hospital?" Arabella asked, as Zack leaned over the bed and rang the bell for a nurse.

"Yes. You had an accident," Lauren said. "You were out in the garden, and a tree blew down—"

"I remember...I was walking the puppy Uncle Zack gave me!" Arabella's cheeks flushed, her eyes brightened, as memories flooded back. "Where is he? Where's my pup?"

Right on cue, Poochie dug his forepaws into the pillow and barked again, a joyful sound. Then, wagging his tail like a metronome, he licked the tip of Arabella's nose as if he thought the chocolate-brown freckles might be edible.

"Aah." Arabella's sigh was tremulous. "There you are, Poochie." She wound her wiry arms around the pup's neck. "Happy New Year," she whispered, snuggling her face into his glossy coat. "And thanks for coming to visit!"

The door swung open and in swept the nurse who had been so outraged at the idea of bringing a dog into the hospital.

She stopped short when she saw the scene before her.

She stared for a long moment, and then her grimly set features softened. She moved to the bed.

"Well," she said to Arabella, "and what have we here?"

Arabella looked at her uncle Zack, and at her aunt Lauren, at her great-aunt Dolly Smith and finally at her dog, Poochie, so cozily nestled in her arms.

Then she looked at the nurse with a beatific smile.

"What we have here," she said, "is a family."

EPILOGUE

Pineapple Villa
Hawaii
March 18

Dear Mrs. Fleetwood,

I'm writing to thank you for looking after Poochie for me. I hope he's being good and not having too many acidents. Hawaii's totally awesome. Aunt Lauren and Uncle Zack took me out on a catamaran this afternoon and then they went to bed. I think the sun makes them real sleepy cos their spending an awful lot of time in their room. That's okay by me cos their leaving me in capible hands like they say. And it's the school break so theirs lots of kids for me to play with. I'm missing Poochie. Tell him I'll be home in one week. And tell him it's lucky Uncle Zack got his cast off last month cos it's great here for swimming.

P.S. Great-Aunt Dolly Smith just read this and said I have a lot of speling mistakes. I told her I don't have a eraser here so she gave her nose a big blow and said it wood have to be all rite then woodent it.

P.P.S. Sorry if this letter has a funny smell. By acident I spilt some of Aunt Lauren's perfume on the paper. In case your intrested its called let me have a look at the bottle Nuit Etoilee. I asked Aunt Lauren what it meant and she said it was French and stood for Starry Night. And then she looked at Uncle Zack and I thought for a minute they were both gonna cry but then he whirled me up and grabbed Aunt Lauren and even Great-Aunt Dolly Smith and said Come on, guys, time for a group hug! And they all squeezed me so hard I thought I was gonna pass out. Don't forget to hug Poochie for me I sure miss him.

Love to you and Mr. Fleetwood and to Poochie of course.

Yours truly,
Arabella Smith Alexander,
Writing to you from Hawaii.

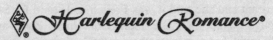

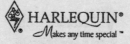

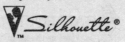

**3 Stories of Holiday Romance from three
bestselling Harlequin® authors**

Valentine Babies
by
ANNE STUART

TARA TAYLOR QUINN

JULE McBRIDE

Goddess in Waiting by Anne Stuart
Edward walks into Marika's funky maternity shop to pick
up some things for his sister. He doesn't expect to assist
in the delivery of a baby and fall for outrageous Marika.

Gabe's Special Delivery by Tara Taylor Quinn
On February 14, Gabe Stone finds a living, breathing
valentine on his doorstep—his daughter. Her mother
has given Gabe four hours to adjust to fatherhood,
resolve custody and win back his ex-wife?

My Man Valentine by Jule McBride
Everyone knows Eloise Hunter and C. D. Valentine
are in love. Except Eloise and C. D. Then, one of
Eloise's baby-sitting clients leaves her with a baby to
mind, and C. D. swings into protector mode.

VALENTINE BABIES
On sale January 2000 at your favorite retail outlet.

HARLEQUIN®
Makes any time special ™

Visit us at www.romance.net

PHVALB

Come escape with Harlequin's new

Series Sampler

Four great full-length Harlequin novels bound together in one fabulous volume and at an unbelievable price.

Be transported back in time with a Harlequin Historical® novel, get caught up in a mystery with Intrigue®, be tempted by a hot, sizzling romance with Harlequin Temptation®, or just enjoy a down-home all-American read with American Romance®.

You won't be able to put this collection down!

On sale February 2000 at your favorite retail outlet.

HARLEQUIN®
Makes any time special ™

Visit us at www.romance.net   PHESC